I0682919

THE BOOK OF QUESTIONS

BOOK 2

THE ADVENTURES OF BOYO

AMY R. HODGSON

ONROX PUBLISHING

This novella is a work of fiction. Characters, names, dialogues, and incidents are the product of the author's imagination. Any resemblance to persons, living or dead, is coincidental.

Copyright © 2022 by Amy R. Hodgson

Second paperback edition May 2025

Illustrations by Silvia Ilona Klatt

ISBN: 979-8-9874852-3-1

Published by OnRox Publishing

www.DiscernAcademy.com

Scan here

to access the online literature courses
for this series and other great novels.

To God be the glory

So many thanks to my beloved family—Charlie, Dakota and Rachel, Tara and Clint—for their support, patience, and constant love. To my grandchildren, Maxx, Bayy, Boone, and Goldynn—the next generation of readers and world-changers. You all make my writing possible and my life joyous.

I am also so thankful for my editing team: Debbie Carroll, Dakota Hodgson, and Erin Knowles. You are invaluable!

Silvia Ilonc Klatt, your artistry blesses us all!

CONTENTS

PROLOGUE

He walked around his dented but faithful silver P-51 Mustang, nodding approval to the ground crew; all looked good. He patted the ferocious image of a black bear stenciled in front of the cockpit—come what may, he was a Mainer!

He'd been up since 3 am with his squadron, eating a quick breakfast and getting a new briefing. Their mission, originally escorting a group of bombers, had been changed to "sweeping" for a lone photo recon plane. Since the Luftwaffe had taken out the last two recon missions, Mustangs were now assigned as armed escorts. Their mission: get the recon plane in and out of Germany so the Allies would have updated photos of troop movements, factory layouts, and the results of the recent bombings. No matter how many enemy planes were shot down, the mission would be a failure if the recon plane did not return to base with the critical intel.

Easing his lanky 6'1" frame into the cockpit, the broad-shouldered pilot wedged himself in the metal cocoon. He didn't mind; the speed and maneuverability of the P-51 outweighed any discomforts. He sweated a bit, but he'd need the warmth at 25,000 feet. Settling in, he smiled at the small photo, a grainy black and white picture of his wife and son, taped on the left side of the console. They were his motiva-

1

tion, always visible but never in the way. Locking the canopy into place, he shut out every distraction and focused only on his mission.

He clicked the radio transmitter: "Black Bear to Squadron, final check! Lock canopy, arm guns after take-off. Form on me. Let's go, boys, like a boomerang! Swift but silent! Out quick and back quick. Watch out for each other; eyes up and hearts strong!"

Radio discipline was strict, but he heard a chorus of static and responses: "Copy that!" "Wilco, Black Bear!" "Roger!" He smiled when he heard his wing man Gator's resounding Alabama-twanged "A-men!"

His eyes swept the horizon, and he regularly twisted his body and head, always checking his six, the blind spot directly behind his tail. Four hours later, cold and weary from their constant vigilance, the squad banked their planes west, toward England. They'd successfully reconned the Rhineland, well hidden by the cloud cover. Thoughts of rest and food fled as the calm scene exploded into chaos at the radio shout: "Hun in the sun! Hun in the sun at 9 o'clock!"

There were too many planes; Gator saw the Black Bear veer sharply out of formation, hoping to lure a German or two away from the recon plane. It worked! Three planes chased his leader into the western clouds. He wanted to follow and help, but the mission came first. Gator said a quick prayer for his friend and then climbed sharply to take advantage of the altitude and help the squad take out the remaining Luftwaffe attackers.

The Black Bear dove low into a thick cloud bank, and his peripheral vision registered glints flashing beside him. Needing to get as far away as possible from the recon plane, he accelerated and zigged in a deadly eastern race, thankful for the speed of his faithful Mustang. Far enough from the recon plane, he pulled the yoke back and started a swift ascent. To save his squad and the mission, he'd made himself the target. Now he was ready to fight. Anger sharpened his vision and flooded his body with strength. His stomach clenched as he threw the plane into a brutally steep descent. The Germans followed, but not with the same surgical, almost supernatural, precision. As one German plane, with its black crosses, overshot him, he pulled up and

2

shot calmly until white smoke billowed out of the front. His odds were better now.

Like most dog fights, it was a slow-motion blur. The second Messerschmitt emptied its tracers; the air erupted in deadly fireworks of green. He stopped thinking and just reacted, his hands directing the plane in upward spirals, always seeking higher altitude. Again, he dropped from above, screaming down to take out the second German with his .50 caliber slugs ripping up the enemy's fuselage.

The third plane, which had stayed just outside of the Black Bear's reach, turned and raced toward the safety of a German home base.

A smile momentarily crossed his face, until he smelled fuel and the engine bucked. The dangers of fire lit up his imagination, so he drove the plane straight down, hoping the power dive would extinguish any possible flames.

Minutes passed and no fire came, but the engine had stopped. He sat in deafening silence, hoping his glide would take him to an open field.

He looked again at the photo. His voice cracked: "I'm so sorry, but I've run out of sky." The ground and trees rushed to fill his vision.

CHAPTER 1

 aine

August 17, 1943

The third time I smashed down was the hardest fall yet. It ripped my jeans and tore up the skin on my knee. After that, I quit trying to run and just limped as fast as I could, never taking my eyes off the lights up ahead. The moonless night made the field treacherous—granite stones were hidden and scattered like land mines. I tried to run but kept tripping over the unseen rocks in the deep darkness. I was finished running away from Grandfather; now I was running away from the menacing sounds in the woods, now I was running toward home.

The lanterns cast a glow around the whole house—it shone with a welcoming beauty. As I got closer, Grandfather appeared to be huddled on the steps; no, I could see he was kneeling. I heard him call my name but I couldn't answer. My throat seized up. Grandfather called again, his arms lifted to the sky, but my answer was just a croak. The third time he called "Boyo," I was able to yell back to him, "Here I am!"

I was still a long way off, but he stood up and ran to me. He hugged my neck. His breath was as ragged and short as mine. "I'm sorry, Grandfather, really I am."

5

But he shook his head, his arm around my shoulders, and said, "Tom Timothy, I'm just so thankful that you are home safely. I have been looking for you, calling your name, and praying. I wanted to go get help from town, but I couldn't leave you alone." He hugged me again. "Where have you been, Boyo, where?"

"I was so upset at dinner, Grandfather, that I ran into the woods to hide. All I could see or hear or think was an angry red. I was lost in my anger, so upset that I couldn't see or think straight—do you know what I mean?" I couldn't see his face in the night, but he squeezed my shoulder, which let me know he understood. "And then I fell asleep in the woods, Grandfather, behind Big Ben[1], and when I awoke, it was pitch black. I couldn't see my own hands. But I could feel the rough bark of Big Ben, no other tree has that size diameter, so I had an idea of where I knelt in the pine needles. I inched my way around the big tree. I was afraid, alone, disoriented, but not lost. No, sir, I was not lost because you lit the way home for me. I tried to run at first, but I kept tripping in the darkness. But I could see my destination, I could see home, my true north. Thank you, Grandfather." And I hugged him back, for the very first time.

We stood in silence for a moment and then walked slowly the rest of the way due to my limp. The house shone with glorious light on that black night, and I felt a sense of peace as I opened the kitchen door. Grandfather had cleaned up from dinner, my usual chore, and he directed me to the wooden bench. "I don't have a fattened calf for you, Tom Timothy, but how about a bowl of berries with cream?"

I hadn't realized I was hungry, but somehow he knew. I nodded yes to the berries and cream but had to ask—"Why would I want a fat calf, Grandfather?"

He looked weary but smiled as he set the blackberries in front of me. "In the Bible, when there was a celebration, a reason for joy and thanksgiving, like a lost son returning to his father, they would have a big feast and eat a special calf that had been fed well and set aside in preparation for a time of rejoicing. A time just like this, Boyo."

I was hungry, and those berries tasted so good that I forgot about my knee and the dark woods. I didn't need to know everything about Mother and Father right now; I just needed to eat and rest. My wilderness experience had left me weak and weary.

6

"Now, let's take a look at that knee, Tom Timothy. What happened? We might need to pay a visit to Miss Rachel[2] if it doesn't clean up well."

"I started running home, Grandfather, but there was no moon tonight. I tripped a few times, always landing on the same knee." I looked down at my left knee; the jeans were torn and bloody. All I could see was dirt mixed with blood, and it was starting to hurt. "I forgot to step high." I stood slowly and removed my jeans while Grandfather warmed water on the stove. He handed me a clean damp cloth to start the cleansing process. I worked slowly, starting on the edges of the cut. Pain and fear of the deepness of the wound caused my hands to shake with trepidation. Now I knew firsthand the meaning of the word gingerly as I used care and caution in wiping away the dried blood and embedded dirt.

But Grandfather soon took over. He tilted his head as he assessed my knee, and I waited with bated breath. Mother had explained to me that bated breath means holding your breath or breathing that is short and shallow due to stress or anxiety. I first thought it had something to do with worms on a hook[3], but she set me straight. Now I was living the phrase; worry seemed to have a tight squeeze on my lungs as I gripped the edges of the bench.

I clenched my jaw and gritted my teeth as Grandfather continued to clean my wound. He finally stood up, and I exhaled a shaky breath. "I'm heading upstairs to get your short pants. Miss Rachel needs to look at that knee. Go wash your hands and face, and I'll get the truck started. It's too late for Balaam[4]."

I took a deep breath and looked down. Yes, that knee was a mess. I figured that soon I'd have a real scar of my own to show Gio[5]. Living in the woods of Maine was certainly an adventure, even a dangerous one at times.

---

1. *Big Ben* is an enormous white pine found in the woods surrounding the farm. It towers over the trees, much like the famous bell tower Big Ben stood tall in London. Naming the tree *Big Ben* is also an example of an allusion.
2. Miss Rachel is a character who was introduced in the first book. She is Grandfather's good friend, the closest neighbor, and a gifted herbal healer.
3. Example of a pun—bated breath is contrasted with "bait" as in worms on a hook.
4. Balaam is the name of Grandfather's horse.
5. Gio is Tom Timothy's best and only friend from New York. Slightly older and quite a fighter, Gio defended Tom Timothy from bullies. Tom Timothy was sent to Maine after Gio was knifed in the stomach by a street gang.

CHAPTER 2

 aine

IT TOOK *Grandfather about ten minutes to meet me in the truck as he had to extinguish all the lanterns before we left—only the fireplace glowed. The house resumed its normal look, well-worn but comfortable.*

Grandfather didn't speak on the slow drive over to Miss Rachel's other than to warn me: "I've got to be careful driving at night this time of year; moose often bust out of the woods, and a moose or even a deer could cause a bad accident." He drove cautiously, focused on the dim area of visibility lit by the headlights.

As we bounced along the rutted road, I sat back on the uncomfortable truck seat, its poking springs helped take my mind off the ache in my knee. This truck was a lot like Grandfather in some ways, I figured. It was rough-looking yet sturdy, useful rather than comfortable, but trustworthy when it counted. I had to admit to myself that my feelings toward Grandfather had really evolved. Either he had changed, or I had—I wasn't sure which.

In the beginning, I knew I wouldn't like him; I didn't plan to hate him, but I certainly had no kind feelings toward a man who had never even

8

acknowledged my existence. What kind of grandfather never visits his family or even writes them a letter? When Mother told me that I had to go to him, to live with him for one hundred days, I was scared and heartsick. I'd read enough fairy tales and stories about evil stepmothers and mean old people; I begged Mother to let me stay. I even promised to lock myself in my room every day, but she wouldn't listen. She was usually open to discussion, yet on the subject of my immediate departure to an unknown, old farmer in Maine, she was adamant, unwilling to change her mind or even talk about it.

The sight of Grandfather at the train station in Augusta frightened me. He was big, bearded, and short of words. I wasn't happy to see him, and he didn't seem thrilled to meet me, his only grandchild. He was grumpy, not wanting to waste time or money, even to send Mother a telegram to let her know I'd arrived safely. Growing up in Brooklyn, I knew Father wasn't rich, but he always had a spare nickel for me. In contrast, Grandfather was the epitome, the very image, of frugality. Gio would probably have called him a penny-pincher until he got to know him. Now, I think they would become friends, Gio and Grandfather, if they ever had the chance to meet. Nothing is better than when your friends are also friends, right? Grandfather once bought me a bag of candy when I was feeling low; I shouldn't forget that!

Grandfather is also a hard worker, a necessity for a saltwater farm, as he always reminds me. At first, I really resented his work ethic because he seemed determined that I share it. Before I came to his farm, I thought keeping my room clean and bed made were more than enough chores. Not any longer! I was proud, when I wasn't complaining—veracity, always veracity[1]—about my garden (which is a third of an acre), about the barn after I'd mucked it, and about the kitchen once I'd cleaned it. I was proud of my calloused hands, a working man's hands according to Grandfather, and my feet that no longer needed shoes.

And I was no longer afraid of Grandfather because I trusted him. Now that was not to say that I didn't fear his anger or his disappointment, I still did, but I knew that I could trust him no matter the circumstances. He would never coddle me like Mother; he expected the best of me, like Father. So, I trusted him and let him teach me the ways of a saltwater farmer. I read the books he recommended, and I listened to the truths he shared. But I didn't always agree with him, yet he let me have questions and my own opinions.

9

At first, I think I was a burden to Grandfather, but we had become more like partners. I knew Mother would be proud of me; however, I wasn't so sure about Father. As I became closer to Grandfather, I wondered if I was betraying Father in some way. As the son of my father, did I have to share his hostilities? I just wasn't certain, but I couldn't ask Grandfather, not yet anyway.

Betrayal and loyalty—how could I not be loyal to Father who loved me and took care of me for nearly ten years, until he had to go to war, and to Grandfather, who had literally saved my life[2] and taught me so much? How could I ever betray either of them? This was my current dilemma.

Thankfully we made it to Miss Rachel's house without encountering any four-legged beasts in the night. Well, her cat Cheshire did meet us on her front steps. Grandfather knocked softly, calling out in a gentle tone, "It's just Joshua and Tom Timothy, Rachel."

It took a moment, but then the door opened, and the smell of herbs floated out. I breathed deeply. It was clear that she wasn't expecting us as she was wrapped up in a robe. Nevertheless, her smile welcomed us into the cozy cottage.

Her eyes quickly spotted the bloody bandage around my knee, and she led me to the hearth. "What have we here, Tom Timothy?" she asked.

As I was a bit embarrassed by my outburst during dinner, I told her a shortened version. "I was running across the field in the dark. I fell down a couple of times, the last time against a jagged rock." I looked toward Grandfather.

"We tried to clean it up, Rachel, but I'm thinking it needs some of your medicine to prevent infection and maybe a few stitches," finished Grandfather.

She nodded and smiled at me. "Well, Tom Timothy, it's poultice time again."

I smiled back, remembering the soothing poultice that took away most of the pain. But the thought of the sharp needle piercing my skin again and again made me wince. Fortitude, I reminded myself again, fortitude[3]!

10

1. Veracity or truthfulness is very important to Tom Timothy; he often catches himself when making excuses or bending the truth and reminds himself of "veracity."
2. In *Boyo*, Grandfather rescued Tom Timothy from drowning.
3. Tom Timothy also often reminds himself to be tough by repeating the word "fortitude."

CHAPTER 3

$\mathcal{M}$aine

I PUSHED AWAY the thought of the stabbing needle and replaced it with the idea of trust, trust and its place in my world. Mother had told me once that the mind can make a hell of heaven or a heaven of hell, just by thinking.[1] So I had the choice to focus my mind on the upcoming pain or to distract myself as best I could. I chose distraction and trust.

Trust was something very precious in my life. I always trusted my parents; not only did they deserve it, but I really had no other choice as a baby and a child. Yes, I always trusted in their love. It gave me a safe home, a refuge from a world that seemed always to stare at me with disgust[2]. Trust was easy and natural with my parents but so foreign with everyone else.

Except my friend, Gio—I could trust him. I knew that he would always defend me. He wasn't perfect, I also knew that, but I thought that Grandfather was wrong. Even though we stole a lot of fruit, Gio didn't make me a worse person. He made me a braver person. It was easier to stand in a storm when you had a friend next to you. Gio always stood by me. When I got home, I would explain to him my new perspective on stealing. After working my garden for nearly three months, I sure would be upset if a bunch of kids

12

came at night and stole my vegetables. Yes, I certainly had a different viewpoint now. That's not even including Grandfather's perspective, his way of looking at everything and everyone through his Bible. He'd say, first of all, stealing is wrong because God says so, and then we'd discuss the ramifications of such a truth. Yes, basically, stealing is wrong, but what if your child is starving?[3] Is it always wrong? Are there extenuating circumstances, situations that would excuse the person? What about Robin Hood stealing from the rich to give to the poor? Grandfather told me it wasn't that simple—there was a corrupt aristocracy, and Robin was helping the good people, even the wealthy ones.

I loved that Grandfather was always willing to discuss the possibilities. Father said that Grandfather was too rigid in his religion, but I didn't see it. Now, Grandfather was certainly steadfast, so firm in his beliefs, but he was always willing to answer my questions and hear my concerns. Wasn't he that way with Father? I wondered.

I also had come to trust Miss Rachel; in fact, she was one of my favorite people in the world, not that I knew that many. The cooling poultice resting on my knee reminded me of her gentleness and kindness. I knew she could have just stitched me up straightaway without any poultice if she were impatient or angry about being disturbed late in the night. No, Miss Rachel was kind and knowledgeable and so quick to help. That was enough to make anyone like her, but I trusted her as well. Before she came back with that needle, I was going to remember why I trusted her so much.

I closed my eyes and breathed deeply: first, I trusted her because Grandfather trusted her, and I trusted him. It was like an overflowing of trust. Second, I trusted her because she fixed my lip so well. And third, I trusted her because she truly cared about me, wanted the best for me. She even shared her favorite books with me. Finally, I trusted her because she said her healing gift was from God, the God of the universe. Those were some impressive credentials if she was right. All in all, there was a lot to trust in Miss Rachel.

Then came the needle.

It didn't matter if your hands were calloused a half inch thick or the soles of your feet could walk on broken clam and mussel shells, a needle hurt! Only Grandfather's hand on my shoulder and my rapidly blinking eyes kept me from crying out. I was so glad when she finished—eight black stitches now decorated my swollen left knee. I took a deep breath and let my muscles relax.

She led me to the table, sat me down on the bench, and put a pillow under my leg. "Well done, Tom Timothy. Keep it elevated tonight."

I had been so busy contemplating the concept of Trust and trying not to cry that I didn't notice Miss Rachel and her toasting fork. As soon as she washed her hands, she placed a buttered piece of her oatmeal toast slathered in lavender honey right in front of me. With one bite left, she gave me another one. Not only did I trust her, but I was very fond of her as well!

Despite the cooling poultice on my knee, the ride home was off to a bumpy start. I couldn't keep my leg elevated, and the ache quickly returned. I closed my eyes and tried to imagine myself in London, racing around the cobblestone streets in a black hansom cab with Sherlock Holmes. The distraction nearly worked until Grandfather slammed on his brakes with the sharp interjection: "Oh Lord!"

I simultaneously cried out in pain and opened my eyes. I froze in astonishment—pain left my mind as I forgot to breathe! Four feet in front of the headlights, bathed in their glow, stood an enormous moose with a huge head full of antlers. It was so big that we were looking up at it! Brown and shaggy, a massive, hunch-backed, muscled body supported the antlers. Two beady dark eyes stared at us, and we could hear its snort of displeasure.

Grandfather whispered. "Don't move or speak, Boyo. That bull's liable to charge us. He looks to be about 1,300 hundred pounds with a full set of antlers. With antlers that size, he's in his prime and might be very aggressive, eager for a fight."

Grandfather didn't need to worry about noise or movement from me—I was stunned. It was enormous, snorting, and dangerous. The moose whipped his head back like Balaam when he was upset.

14

"Look closely, Boyo," Grandfather continued to whisper without moving. "See how his fur stands up along the back of its neck and hump, like a dog's when it is getting ready to attack. And his ears are laid flat back against his head, another sign of aggression. Hold fast, Tom Timothy, hold fast!"

---

1. The reference is to John Milton's *Paradise Lost:* "The mind is its own place, it can make heaven out of hell or hell out of heaven."
2. Remember that Tom Timothy suffered from a cleft palate which embarrassed him and made him very self-conscious. Through prayer and skill, Miss Rachel healed him and removed most of the ugly scar.
3. This is the dilemma of Jean Valjean in *Les Misérables*—steal some bread or let a child starve.

CHAPTER 4

$\mathcal{M}$aine

THAT BULL MOOSE moved so fast that it was a blur, a bone-jarring and night-shattering blur. I couldn't tell whether his shoulder or his antlers hit the truck first, but it didn't matter. That poor old truck shook like a mouse caught between the teeth of a cat. We were just as helpless as that rodent. I had braced myself against the door and the dashboard, but still I was tossed into Grandfather and slammed against the back window. Hiding behind my hands, I saw the moose rear up and slam down its front hooves. The crunch of the hood was frighteningly loud, and the headlights quickly dimmed. Grandfather's arm gripped me tightly around my shoulders, and we waited silently for the second attack. It was deathly silent, but then I heard another snort. I tightened my muscles and held my breath, bracing myself. Just when I finally relaxed and exhaled, that beast struck again, and the truck shook mightily, rattling my teeth in my head. I'd never felt such power. Grandfather held me firmly. We both initially flinched when we heard the moose crashing through the brush on the left side of the truck, but our tension diminished as the sounds receded. We waited, listening for any sounds; it was

16

nerve-wracking. Silence finally returned to the darkness; only one feeble headlight still worked, but it looked clear in front of us.

Grandfather exhaled loudly. "Well, Tom Timothy, let's check the damage. This old truck has been through a lot—let's just hope it has survived this moose encounter and can get us home!"

"But, Grandfather, wait! That moose..." I pulled against his arm, keeping him in the truck. No human could stand against that creature!

"It's okay, Tom Timothy. We heard him leave the area about five minutes ago. One thing about moose is they are not always stealthy; you can usually hear them coming. Listen carefully. Now, the crickets and night creatures are making noise again—it's safe. I'm sure." He loosened my fingers and stepped into the darkness.

Wary, with all my senses on high alert, I began to slowly inch out of the truck cab.

"Stay by the door, Tom Timothy. There's broken glass from the headlight all over the road. Throw me some gloves. I've got to clear it away from the tires, or we'll end up spending the night right here."

I hurriedly searched the cab and found his thick leather gloves crammed into the glove compartment. Carefully edging to the front of the truck, I leaned around to look. What a mess! The whole front of the cab was smashed, crumpled like a tin can that met a heavy hammer. One headlight was shattered; all over the road slivers of glass glimmered. Grandfather stood with his hands on his hips, surveying the damage. For once, I was glad we drove such a junker—imagine how horrible it would have been if the truck were new! Then I felt bad; that old truck was all that had been between me and a crazy, killer moose. Why, it looked like that beast had been aiming right for me!

I quickly tossed Grandfather the gloves. Sleeping in the truck tonight, surrounded by who knows what aggressive creatures, was an adventure I was eager to skip.

"Thanks, Boyo. Now, can you reach the rake and basket in the back?"

"Why, Grandfather? Can't we just get out of here? Now? We can come back in the daylight."

"Well, Tom Timothy, we don't want Miss Rachel to drive over this glass and be stuck out here with a flat, do we? And what about animals? This glass could slice up an unsuspecting creature pretty quickly." He glanced toward

17

me. "They can handle God's sharp granite rocks, but not necessarily the glass or metal discarded by men. I think we need to clean up our mess, don't you?"

I mumbled and limped toward the back of the truck. Seemed to me that the mess belonged to the moose, not to me. But this was one time it wouldn't do to argue with Grandfather—he was mighty particular about anything concerning Miss Rachel.

I dropped the rusty truck gate and hoisted myself up, scooting backwards until I felt the rake and basket. I then dragged them with me as I scooted forwards. Trying to keep my left knee straight was slowing me down, and it was aching again, so I took my time. When I limped back to Grandfather with his requests, he had the hood open. I doubted he could see much, as there was barely a sliver of the moon now. Thankfully, there were no sounds of the moose returning.

"Hop back in the truck, Boyo. I'll have this metal and glass raked up in no time, and then we'll head for home. I think this old guy will get us home." He patted the hood after he slammed it shut.

I winced at the noise as it reverberated through the night and hauled myself back up into the truck. I stretched my leg across the seat and thought about that moose. What would it have done if we'd gone to Miss Rachel's with Balaam instead of driving the truck? I started sweating thinking about it. That wagon couldn't have protected us! Would it have killed Balaam and us? Why hadn't Grandfather warned me about moose before? My fear was now becoming colored by anger. Those antlers were huge, and they would have crushed me!

Although I knew that the only reason we were out tonight was because I'd hurt my leg, I was still angry. With a creature that big, how could we protect ourselves? It wasn't fair. Gio always said, "Life ain't fair," and now I saw his point. How could I ever walk the woods again? Or ride to Miss Rachel's in the wagon? I felt like I'd felt after that gang beat us up in that Brooklyn alley. I was vulnerable, and it made me scared and angry. I thought I was done hiding when I came to Grandfather's farm. I thought my days of fear were over. These thoughts crowded into the truck with me, and I was helpless against them.

When Grandfather finished clearing the road, he put the rake back into the truck bed. But then he carefully placed the basket of broken glass and twisted metal on the floor in front of me. I looked at the basket with wicked shards of glass pointing at me and turned to him. "Grandfather!"

His calm response of "Yes?" infuriated me.

"Grandfather! What if that moose attacks me again? I'll be crushed into the broken glass and metal! Why, Miss Rachel won't have enough stitches to save me!"

He took his hand away from the key and looked at me closely. He picked up the basket and placed it in the truck bed. When he sat again in the truck he asked, "What's wrong, Boyo? That moose isn't coming back. He wasn't attacking you personally, you know. He felt the truck was invading his territory. You're okay." He patted my shoulder.

"Okay? We are not okay, Grandfather. We were nearly killed!" I shook off his hand. I was breathing heavily but couldn't stop my words. I was angry— angry and afraid.

"You talk about God, your God, who is omnipotent and loving. Well, where was he tonight? Huh? Why did he let this happen? Why does he let bad things happen, any bad things? Why did Father have to go to war? What kind of God is he?" My voice dropped to a whisper: "He didn't protect us. He didn't protect Gio! What if he doesn't protect Father?"

"Those are hard questions, Tom Timothy," began Grandfather.

"Please stop, please, Grandfather. I don't want to talk anymore tonight. Just take me home."

He nodded slowly, then turned his eyes back to the road and started the truck. We seemed to creep slowly back to the farmhouse, in a dim haze, threatened by the dark surrounding us.

Grandfather lit a lantern and walked with me to the outhouse. Was he afraid too? Then, he helped me up the stairs to my room because my knee hurt in its stiffness, and the stitches were pulling sharply.

He went downstairs as I changed into my nightclothes and crawled under the covers. Would I even be able to sleep tonight? The world and all its hidden evils seemed to crouch around the house, ready to charge me like that moose. My heart pounded.

Grandfather came quietly into the room and put a cup in my hands. I was thankful for its heat. "It's a warm cup of milk and honey, Tom Timothy. Drink it and rest." Somehow, Grandfather's drink tasted like peace might taste. He placed his hand on my head—I felt its weight. "Be strong and coura-

19

geous! Do not tremble and be dismayed,"[1] *he hesitated, as though he would say more. But he didn't. He just smiled down at me, turned down the lantern so it was barely a glimmer, and left the room.*

---

1. Joshua 1:9 – Have I not commanded you? Be strong and courageous. Do not be frightened, and do not be dismayed, for the Lord your God is with you wherever you go."

CHAPTER 5

$\mathcal{N}$ew York City

NIGHT HAD ALSO FALLEN in Brooklyn, and a similar fear and despair filled the atmosphere. It wasn't an ugly room, just dismal; the four walls seemed to trap years of loneliness left by dispirited boarders. The comforting beauty Ruth remembered from the old apartment in the crowded but cheerful tenement had not survived the quarter mile move.

She sat on a hard wooden chair that matched none of the other sparse furniture and used a stack of boxes as a makeshift desk. Deep sighs punctuated her writing; at times her pen trembled.

My Dearest Tom,

This is always the hardest time for me, just before sleep. My imagination runs wild, and I have no distractions to drive away my fears. It has been over four months since your last letter, and thirty days since the

21

telegram declaring you "Missing in Action." What does that even mean, Tom? How can you be lost? I haven't told Tom Timothy anything yet. What is there to tell? His father is lost? No, I won't tell him! And the summer is close to ending—how can the seasons continue in their pattern while our world is frozen?

Lines for food here are so long, but I have no appetite. On your father's farm, Tom Timothy has plenty to eat, don't worry. I force myself to eat because I know you must still be alive. I know because my heart has not completely shattered.

I've moved out of the apartment and taken a room at the boardinghouse, Mrs. Shaw's Rooming House, down the street. I don't need the space now that Tom Timothy is gone, but I kept all your books, of course, and Tom Timothy's favorite toys. The apartment was too expensive and too empty. This room is all I need now. I'm saving the extra rent money in war bonds at the bank on the corner. I'm saving for Tom Timothy's education and for the unknown future that haunts me.

Tom Timothy is still with your father, and his letters sound like he is well and enjoying himself. I miss him terribly, Tom, but I don't want him to see me so lost and broken. I fear I might frighten him. I think you would have agreed to send him to Maine, if we could only have spoken.

The last time I was this broken, you were there to lift me up and hold me. You helped me heal. The darkness is encroaching, hiding even my happy memories.

22

Tom, please come home, darling, please.

Always your loving Ruth

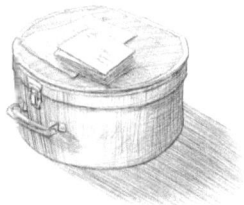

She wiped away her tears and placed the letter on top of the stack of other unsent letters in a faded, green felt hatbox. It made no sense to waste money on postage stamps, as no one knew where he was, but she couldn't stop writing him. She had to keep the faith, faith in her husband coming home, faith in her family reuniting, any kind of faith at this point. As she replaced the box lid, she broke down completely, sobbing breathlessly. She hugged herself and rocked back and forth, pitifully thin in her worn nightgown. Every night, she tried to write away her fears and pain, but it was rarely effective; it was just a feeble gate that failed to corral the nightmare of a life without Tom.

Her only refuge was the past, memories of her times with Tom. They'd met at the university, in a crowded Orono lecture hall that smelled of wet wool and too many humans. She had been drawn to his strength, broad shoulders that had lifted much, hands that knew work. Yet there was a tenderness and brittleness that battled in him for as long as she'd known him. They immediately recognized a shared intellectual curiosity. It was a strong initial attraction, fuel to a fire, helpful in battling the cold Maine winter and alleviating her concerns about her first year of college.

Recently orphaned, Ruth welcomed his growing presence in her life. Tom made her feel safe and valuable. In his arms, she found refuge. He helped assuage, to soften and gently wipe away, the painful loneliness after her parents' death. Her only concern about Tom was

23

his estrangement from his father. She knew about his mother who had recently passed—Tom talked a little about her, always in the terms of an adoring only son who was devastated by her death; he gave few particulars. Tom dismissed any mention of his father: "There's nothing to discuss, Ruth, nothing." So, their wedding was small, just the justice of the peace and two classmates as witnesses.

It had been so simple then, so clear. *Do you take this man to be your lawfully wedded husband?* Her "yes" had been immediate and sincere. There was no doubt in her mind and heart that Tom was her man for life. But now there were questions, too many questions. Where was Tom? What would become of Tom Timothy? Was she strong enough to continue without Tom? Hadn't she suffered enough? Hadn't they lost enough? What more did God want from her? She wanted to scream, but she hadn't the strength, and it was against the boarding-house rules posted on the inside of her room.

- **No male visitors permitted within this room**
- **No smoking**
- **No use of electrical appliances**
- **No noise that can be heard outside your room, singing included**
- **No food in your room**
- **All doors locked at 10 pm**

It almost made her laugh—the ridiculousness of boardinghouse rules when her love was lost, adrift among guns, bombs, and vicious men.

When there were no tears left, she stood and began to walk in a small circle around the room. She lightly brushed her finger over the stacks of books, Tom's Engineering, Forestry, and Piloting manuals. On her second circuit of the room, she clasped a small teddy bear to her chest, like a cherished infant. She continued her pilgrimage in the dingy room, touching each of Tom Timothy's precious tin soldiers like a talisman. The ritual walk helped her compose herself, to quiet the fear and questions.

Finally, she sat down and picked up the pen and another sheet of paper. Her letters to her husband were emotional, barely controlled, but her letters to her son were different. They had to be cheerful and composed, protective of his innocence at all costs. She and Tom had made that decision years ago; they promised each other to spare the boy from their loss. Had they been wise to shield him? They had tried to keep him safe, but at what cost? Would he be able to face the world that she and Tom now knew, a broken and uncertain future? Could she keep that promise, she wondered? These letters with their essential intentionality exhausted her mind as she sought the pleasant phrases, quirky vocabulary, and memorable images the boy would like, and all with a patina of cheerfulness. She couldn't let her pain show. There was so much that she didn't dare tell him, things she didn't even understand herself.

My Dear Tom Timothy,

I'm so glad you are a masterful gardener—I can only imagine the plethora of colorful vegetables that you are stewarding so well. Enjoy them, as North York City has long food lines and a shortage of all vegetables except potatoes! People look like mannequins as they wait stoically in the long lines to cash in their ration cards. Don't worry, I rarely have to wait in the queue.

Gio's mother, however, is frustrated at the lack of tomatoes and onions—her sauces are suffering. Dante is becoming quite the little chatterbox, and he can even coax a smile or two from Gio. The doctor has promised Gio that he'll soon be walking, ambulatory once again. I miss hearing him clattering up and down the stairs.

Father's letters are still delayed; such massive happenings in that part of the world will necessarily impede the delivery of mail to civilians. Please keep him in your prayers; I know how much you miss him.

I'm keeping busy at the factory- your mother making bullets-now that is something to envision and ponder!

Much love and many hugs,
MOTHER

She hoped that her son wouldn't notice that she'd made no mention of his return to New York City; his one hundred days in Maine were nearing an end. There was no life for him here now, she knew. Why, her only social life was a weekly visit to Gio's apartment to gather information to send to Tom Timothy. The rest of her day was working to avoid thinking. She quickly sealed and stamped the letter, putting it in her purse for tomorrow.

She began to pace again, her thoughts even more troubled, if possible, as she considered the next letter she had to write, and to a man she'd never even met.

At least she could address him by his first name; he'd asked her to in his last letter. She was so indebted to him—what was one more request? He already had her greatest treasure; she'd freely given it, actually thrust it upon him. "Oh God, what am I doing?" she felt her prayer linger briefly in the room and then evaporate, useless in the atmosphere of despair. She tried to walk away from her horrified thoughts, but the room wasn't large enough.

She slipped to the floor as she berated herself: "What kind of mother are you? Did you ever even deserve him? Without Tom, you are nothing, less than nothing, useful to no one." Her thoughts and words were merciless, beating her spirit and crushing any remaining hope. "Do it, give him a chance without you!"[1] Her despair hung heavy in the room, like the sickening fog wafting off a polluted river.

She grabbed the pen and wrote furiously, her handwriting wild. In her desperation, the paper was crumpled, pierced in places by her frantic writing. She addressed the envelope with the same wild script,

26

the stamp askew in the upper corner. She grabbed her key and coat and rushed out into the night. She would not, could not wait.

In the darkness, she hurried to the corner, barely able to find the faded red top with its rusted white letters calling for "MAIL." Lifting the bar to open the slot was a more difficult task than she had expected, but she pushed both envelopes into the mailbox and felt her will immediately weaken, as though she'd let fall an essential part of her soul as well. She stumbled back to her room, dropping her coat inside her door. She wept herself to sleep that night, remembering every loss she'd ever known.

---

1. Reminiscent of Bunyan's *The Pilgrim's Progress* when Christian and Hopeful are trapped in Doubting Castle of Despond and severely beaten by Giant Despair—Christian's depression nearly destroys him.

CHAPTER 6

$\mathcal{M}$aine

August 18, 1943

Because I was supposed to rest my knee for a few days, I was restarting my journal.[1] I had time now to practice my writing, and I wanted to describe some key scenes at Grandfather's farm before I left.

When I heard Grandfather's steady, heavy tread on the stairs, I curled up on my side and closed my eyes. I wasn't ready for any conversations. He paused in the doorway, and then he quietly came in. I could feel him looking at me, but I couldn't hear the words he was mumbling. He finally left, placing something on the small table next to my bed. I waited until I heard him at the bottom of the stairs, then I opened my eyes.

Food. He'd brought me breakfast like there was nothing wrong! Like I wanted to eat after all that happened last night! The anger started to rise in me again, anger still stained by fear. I pulled the covers over my head to shut out the sight and the smell.

But it did smell good. Veracity! My body betrayed me as my stomach growled. All I'd had for supper last night was a bowl of berries. The bacon, eggs, honey-toast, and coffee were so tempting. But it wasn't the food's fault I was angry, and I shouldn't be wasteful. I was a little embarrassed as I

28

devoured it—delicious! Father always said that hunger was the world's best seasoning.

After eating, I knew that it was time to think, to come to terms with my situation. I lay back and assessed. First off, there was no doubt that my knee was aching. Miss Rachel had said to rest it for three days, so some time in bed today was a good start. Eight stitches, I pulled back the sheet to look. Lifting the edge of the bandages, I saw eight neat, black sutures, that's what Miss Rachel called them, lined up across my knee. My knee looked like I felt: red and angry, inflamed.

Now that was something to think about—my leg looked angry about the stitches, which happened when I tripped in the darkness, an accident. I knew I was angry because of the moose attack, which also happened in the darkness, another accident. Both accidents were dangerous, especially to me. So, whose fault was it? Mine? Grandfather's? Or God's? That was really the question I had for Grandfather—whose fault?

My one hundred days in Maine were nearly over, and I wanted to keep a good relationship with Grandfather, but I really needed him to answer that question. I mean, what good was a god who couldn't or wouldn't protect you?

After I hobbled down to the kitchen, my knee was pretty stiff for stairs. Grandfather was gone. He'd gone to the fields, I was sure. It was getting closer to harvest time, so he needed to check everywhere. I knew he couldn't harvest everything himself, with just Balaam, so when I'd asked him his plan last week, he said, "I'll do most of it myself, Boyo, but I'll also trade some time with a few friends from the other farms." I guess that was a good way to share the labor, but I bet Grandfather wished he had a son or grandson to help him with the farm like most of the men from church.

I washed my dishes, visited the privy, and sat on the porch to think. I'd be heading back to New York soon; I'd stopped counting the days, but I could see and feel the subtle signs of summer's exit—a spark of red leaves tucked in among the green, and the need for a quilt some nights.

I stood and walked over to my garden and noted my handiwork and nature's changes: the strong green stalks were noticeably thin, with only a few tomatoes remaining, bright red and ready to eat; the melons' tendrils were drying out, a hint that the melons were nearly finished growing; the cucumber skins were smooth now—I should pick a batch for Miss Rachel to pickle this week. The potato tops were dying off, a sign that the potato skins

29

were toughening, getting ready to be stored for the winter. There should be more than enough for Grandfather and his chowdah; the onion tops were flopping, promising full-grown onions beneath the soil which could be dug up any time. It was funny how I'd learned to communicate with my garden this summer; Gio would enjoy hearing about it. Maybe I could take him and Dante one of my melons?

But what about the late vegetables that Grandfather mentioned? Peppers would grow until the frosts of November, and garlic needed to be planted for next year. My pumpkins—they weren't close to ready yet! Leaving this garden would be hard; I used to hate its constant demands for watering and weeding, but I saw its gifts now. I would miss it; I hoped Grandfather had time to take care of it—it sure looked a lot better since I'd come.

Miss Rachel's directions were clear: "Rest, Tom Timothy, for three days. Give your body a chance to heal; the knee is a tricky injury, so take it easy. No work for him, Joshua, three days off!" But I bet she'd understand that I couldn't just stay in the house. If I walked slowly down to the shore, I'm sure Miss Rachel would consider it resting if I went carefully. I wanted to hear the ocean breathing and smell the freshness. No New York water smelled that good, so sharp and pine-scrubbed!

Grandfather wouldn't be back until past noon, so there was no need to leave a note. I put some crackers in my pocket and filled my canteen. I went slowly down the steps, just like I should. If I locked my knee when I walked, why I couldn't even feel the stitches pulling. It was a fun way to walk until I felt like a soldier marching, and that made me worry again about Father. I didn't want any more questions or worries this morning, so I shook them out of my head and pointed myself toward the water.

---

1. Tom Timothy wants to be a journalist, specifically a war correspondent; as a result, he keeps a journal and works on developing his vocabulary all the time.

CHAPTER 7

Germany

HE AWOKE to cold and darkness, his head throbbing, his body hurting more than he'd imagined it could. His legs responded, but the pain that shot through his left arm stole his breath. He tried not to groan, but the sound forced its way through his parched lips. But then he noticed: it wasn't silent—heavy bodies moved above him, and a rich smell taunted his memories. His hand brushed against a rough woolen blanket, and he pulled the musty cloth over his shivering torso. He must sleep, he told himself, or else the images would drive him mad.

When he awoke again, the cold and darkness still surrounded him, but slivers of light shone above his head. Dirt and dust fell through the cracks, as the heavy noise continued above him. He inhaled deeply through his nose and concentrated on the smell: musky, earthy, slightly sweet. Cattle! There were cows above him! Why had it taken him so long to remember their rich, distinctive smell? He'd grown up on a farm and milked and mucked for nearly two decades. But cows, their placid natures and pastoral images, had no place in his world

31

today, this arena of war and death. "I'm a fighter pilot, a United States P-51 Mustang pilot" he exclaimed to himself in a whisper. "Why am I under a barn?" It was an incongruous thought, but it seemed in concert with the images that he kept driving away from his consciousness.

Rather than dwell on the horrid pictures in his mind, he chose to investigate his surroundings instead. Lying flat on his back, he rotated his eyes. It looked to be a small dark pen of sorts, dirt floor, dirty blanket, a wooden slat ceiling for him as well as floor for the cattle. This was no prison that he'd ever heard of.

"Hello!" he whispered, but there was no human response. He'd been warned of the German POW camps, but never was there a description of something like this.

He took a breath and thought back on his training: time for personal injury assessment. He could move his legs, but the nerves in his left arm screamed of an injury. He put his right hand to his head—his helmet, goggles, and O2 mask were gone. His hand went to his chest where his heart was pounding—no gear whatsoever. He knew he had flown with a B-52 life preserver over his B15 jacket. No wonder he was cold—he was stripped to his skivvies! Even his gloves and boots were gone. His hand flew to his neck; he choked as he realized his dog tags and "blood chit" were gone.[1] There went his hopes of any humane treatment due to the Hague Conventions[2] and its rules.

And his family—without his tags, they'd never know what happened to him. He fought the rising despair and promised himself that he'd fight, he'd fight to live and get back home to Ruth and his boy.

But where was he? In order to get home, he'd need to know where to start. All his maps were in his jacket and plane. His plane? What had happened? His thoughts were disjointed and his memory a blur; he must have a concussion. He must have crashed and suffered a concussion. Yes, that made sense. But stripped down and lying under a barn? That made no sense, nor did the kaleidoscope of images that kept flashing through his mind.

Enemy fire—he remembered the flak guns exploding the clouds around him, and the bullets smashing into his plane. He'd tried to

32

dodge them and thought he'd won the dog fight lottery again. But no, one stray bullet must have hit the coolant tube, the Achilles heel[3] of the P-51 Mustang! What a cursedly lucky hit for the Germans! He'd lost altitude and soon control—he remembered fields, farming fields like he'd worked as a boy; he aimed for those fields and pain shot through his left arm as he experienced again the horror of the crash. When he hit the field, his body tore against the harness, his breath forced from his lungs, like a sucker punch to his gut. How did his ligaments even hold together? It was a wonder, no? A fearful wonder that he had survived. He couldn't honestly call it a crash landing—it was just a crash. A jumble of sound, smells, and colors overwhelmed his senses: burning flesh, manure, German words, staccato blasts of light and fire. His breath quickened as adrenaline flooded his system. "Oh, god," he groaned, "oh, god."

His mind couldn't handle the images nor his body the pain, and he slipped again into unconsciousness.

Light still trickled through the floorboards over his head when he regained consciousness. Unfortunately, it wasn't just a bad dream. It was real. He was hurt, under a barn, with nothing, no identity. He was no one. It was too easy for a "no one" to disappear during this war.

Recalling his promise to fight for his life, he forced himself into a sitting position, leaning heavily on his right arm. His hand touched something, and he pulled back in fear. When it didn't move, he looked more closely. It was a Bible, the Bible he'd kept with him on every mission. "Are you kidding me? They take everything from me and leave only an ancient book of stories? What good will you do me?" he swore at the book.

He realized that the anger had helped clear his mind, so he continued his inspection of the cell. It had to be a prison cell, in some bizarre type of jail.

In the dimness, he could see his body, and he felt great relief when he was able to move his legs and head with only minimal discomfort. That's from the crash, he figured. He slowly turned his head toward his left arm, but it was too dark to see much. His left shoulder was crusty with dirt and dried blood, but his arm was still sticky. At least

33

the heavy bleeding seemed to have stopped. He sat up higher and breathed deeply.

Something lay at the end of the cell, half a dozen inches away from his feet. He peered intently. Whatever it was, a rough cloth covered it. For a moment, his imagination ran away from him, and he feared what horror might be hidden under the cloth. *Don't be ridiculous*, he chided himself. *Don't waste your emotions or energy now; I'm sure there will be plenty to fear later.*

Dizzy and aching, he moved slowly to his knees and leaned over the mystery. He lifted the cloth carefully. Could he trust his eyes?

He grabbed the small jug and forced himself to sip, to sip slowly. Water! It tasted clean. He sipped again and then held the precious vessel to his chest. He must be alive if he could drink water. Carefully setting the jug to the side, he looked again and saw a hunk of dark brown bread. He grabbed these treasures tightly to his chest and blinked back tears of gratitude. Sipping and chewing slowly, Tom soon finished the tastiest meal of his life.

---

1. The blood chit was written in eight languages and stated: "I'm an American aviator and my plane has been destroyed." It also said that if the person who finds the American would help save his life, the American government would financially reward him.
2. International laws that were supposed to protect prisoners of war; they were often disregarded during WW2.
3. An allusion to the Greek myth about the hero Achilles and his one vulnerable spot —his heel.

CHAPTER 8

 ermany

He lay back on the dirt floor, his thirst and hunger temporarily satisfied. His thinking was clearer now—he must remember what happened, what was real and what was just a nightmare. Not only must he remember what happened, but he also must remember who he was. Name, rank, and serial number wasn't enough. He was Tom, beloved of Ruth, father of Tom Timothy, son of ... Tears threatened to break out, and he feared he could never stop the flow once it started. Consciousness was like a murky swamp, dank and not the crystal ocean air of his father's farm, but it didn't matter; he must persevere.

35

It was obvious that he had crashed his plane in Germany—he'd miss that Mustang, the dented silver ridge runner who'd endured so much with him. At lonely times, he'd talked aloud to his plane, sharing his loneliness, his desire and longing for Ruth, his dreams for his little boy. For the past two years, that plane had been a safe, uncomfortable but reliable, second home. He knew that they had been on a run into southern Germany, escorting the recon plane. The dog fight hadn't been going well, so he'd peeled off, to distract at least two or three of the Luftwaffe's attackers. It had worked. The hopelessness of his current situation was only lessened by the knowledge that the men in his squadron, his war-time brothers, had escaped due to his actions. He heard his father's voice, a deep rumble quoting the Bible about laying down his life for his friends[1]; Tom deliberately filled his mind with his own version of truth, the logic of sacrificing one man rather than many.

How could he be sweating in this cold, damp cell? He pulled the worn woolen blanket to his chin.

But what about the other images, the blurry nightmare hallucinations that invaded his memory? He was certain he could remember someone grabbing his arms and pulling him out of the cockpit. His arm throbbed at the memory—it must have been sliced open by the cockpit glass. He could smell the fuel from his plane, and the heat was searing. In fact, it was all a scene from hell. Maybe there was a hell after all, and here it is! *Stop!* he told himself. *I cannot give in to despair, not now. Logic must prevail now more than ever.* He slowed his breathing and controlled his body's shaking.

He closed his eyes, forcing his memory back, back to being

36

dragged from the cockpit. But then he was moved, taken away from the heat of the plane. And then out of the darkness, hands took hold of his dog tags and his blood chit, trying to lift them from his neck. He fought back with his right hand, trying to save his identity. *"Nein!"*[2] came from his attacker, *"nein!"* Tom remembered holding fast until a fist loomed in his eyes and a blow connected with his chin. He touched his jaw—yes, he'd been punched out. *But I saw your face, and I'll never forget it. I will have my revenge, you thief! You coward, hitting an injured man,* Tom whispered to himself.

Tom continued his self-analysis: *So I crashed, was pulled from my plane, taken away from the aircraft, robbed, and then knocked out. Now I'm imprisoned under a barn. Why didn't they just kill me?* He knew the stories of airmen being executed by soldiers who had no compassion and were tired of caring for POWs. Were they just saving him for revenge later? His breathing quickened, but again he demanded logic from himself. Though the thought chilled his very being, he could even understand the lynching of airmen who crashed behind enemy lines after delivering their payloads of explosives. War had revealed such a brutal side of man, and despite conventions and laws, very few nations fought fairly. He knew he had more memories and more questions, but his head was throbbing. He took a final sip from the jug and just hoped it would be refilled soon.

Look on the bright side, he encouraged himself. He was still alive, and he had shelter, strange shelter, but shelter nonetheless. He could sleep easily now, he thought. He didn't need much more, just some straw, clothes, and a pillow. He closed his eyes, proud of his logical approach to this horrifying situation. But the sudden tromp of boots above shattered the stillness and frightened the cows. The violent pounding overwhelmed him with fear, driving away his fleeting moment of optimism. There were men above him, shouting in German, slamming what sounded like rifle butts and throwing farm tools. Angry shouting by several voices and then one calm reply—that is all he could distinguish.

When would they come for him? What would they do? Tension shredded his already exhausted nerves. There was a momentary silence, and then he heard a gun cock. Its blast splintered his small

37

world, and he could barely keep from screaming. He curled into the fetal position, covering his ears and rocking, his mouth forming the prayers he was not even conscious of to a God he no longer acknowledged. When he thought he could bear no more, the boots stomped off into the distance, and a calm returned to the barn. He strained to hear what was happening, if anyone was coming for him, but then he heard it: the ding against the metal bucket, the universal sound of milking. Milking? Milking in the middle of hell? He began to laugh silently but hysterically. Milking!

He was startled when a foot slammed on the floor and a guttural voice whispered, *"Gott im Himmel, leise bitte, leise bitte!"*[3]

He cursed himself for not learning German in school—he only knew a few phrases. *Gott im Himmel* was clear enough, and *bitte* meant please, he was sure of it. Someone was imploring him to do something. Perhaps he had not been laughing silently after all. He started to respond, when he heard a loud shushing sound and solid pats on the cow's flank. A sharp query came from outside the barn, but the voice above him was calm in its answer. Tom knew he must remain silent for now, perhaps for a very long time. He pulled the blanket tight and shut his eyes tighter.

---

1. John 15:13 "Greater love has no one than this, that someone lay down his life for his friends" (ESV).
2. In German: "No!"
3. In German: "God in Heaven, quiet please, quiet please!

CHAPTER 9

 aine

Standing at the top of the bluff, I could see only the shore, ocean, and horizon. It was a taste of infinity, as Grandfather says. I felt small in some ways, but so powerful, maybe like a king looking over his realm. I knew I didn't own the ocean, but no one really does, so I just claimed what I saw, like the early explorers.

The waves kept coming, rising and falling, but always coming to the shore. Sometimes the waves were large, sometimes small, sometimes violent, sometimes peaceful, but always, they came to the shore. Was that an example of eternity, the never ceasing waves of the ocean? It gave me shivers! Now I felt not just small but also temporary, still the king though!

I needed to breathe deeply, fill my lungs with this clean salty air; I had to remember these smells when I walked past the alleys and garbage heaps in the city. Sometimes, the smells of Brooklyn were overwhelming, especially in the summer. Too many people, too much trash, just too much.

I wondered what Maine looks like in the winter. I bet the snow stayed white. New York got so dark and dirty, even the ice turned gray. A fresh snow

39

fall stayed clean and white only for a few hours. The city soon conquered the beauty.

And the fall? It must be something—there were so many trees here on Grandfather's farm! I bet there was a jumble of colors, a patchwork. Orange pumpkins in the garden and all the colors of autumn filling the forest; parks looked pretty in the city, but here, I bet the whole world was autumn.

The water was a lighter blue than usual, and there were only softly rolling waves. It'd be a good time to take out the skiff, if I knew how to swim and my knee were healed. No, I was just going to sit up here, looking down over my kingdom. I would have a couple crackers and a sip or two of water.

I closed my eyes and felt the sun on my face; it was gently warm today. I didn't remember weather like this in the city. It was usually blazing hot, freezing cold, rainy, or windy. Up here on the shore, the weather felt friendly. I was going to miss this spot. I was going to write all this down so that I wouldn't lose this place.

I couldn't help but hear the sea breathing, but it, too, was gentle, like a peaceful sleep—in and out, in and out. I could hear the waves, just a few seagulls, and a soft wind playing with the leaves of the poplars. In the city, I would be hearing streetcars and sirens, people shouting and children playing. It was too loud there to even hear the pigeons, except very early in the morning. I wondered: in Maine, I heard nature calling to me and teaching me, but in New York, I only heard people and manmade things, warning and threatening me. But Mother was in the city, and I knew she needed me, Gio too.

I didn't hear Grandfather until he neared the top. "Are you feeling better, Tom Timothy?"

For a moment, I had forgotten my anger. "Yes, I'm just storing up sights, smells, and sounds to take back to New York."

"It's a good spot for such collections," said Grandfather as he sat beside me. "I come here sometimes too."

"Why would you need to save anything? You never go anywhere."

Grandfather laughed. "I come here to rest. To be still and know that He is God."

The god thing again, I thought to myself. My resentment returned. "You know, Grandfather, I still don't want to talk about a god that isn't dependable or trustworthy. I just don't." I crossed my arms against my chest and stared at the horizon.

"Still angry, are you?" He didn't wait for an answer. "Do you really think that I would serve an undependable, untrustworthy king? Boyo, don't you know me by now?" He stood. "When you are ready, we can talk. I'm heading back to the cornfield. I've left you some stew on the stove; it's still warm."

I didn't watch him walk away—he was sure stubborn about his God. I was beginning to see Father's point of view. Science was dependable: gravity and the rules of nature, like the tides and the seasons. Much more dependable —why, I would bet that when I learned more Science, I would even be free of the scary parts of nature, like infinity and eternity. Those concepts were too big for any boy, or man probably. I mean, with eternity and infinity the ocean and the world itself seemed uncontrollable, and honestly, that made me fearful. It was all too big, too powerful, too awesome for me.

I had to stop thinking such thoughts and enjoy the day instead. Soon, Bethel Farm would only be a memory. I wondered if I'd get to visit again next summer. I'd need to write Grandfather after I left; I was sure he'd be lonely without me.

An eagle! He had such a unique call that I'd know it anywhere. There he was soaring, so high and free. Watching him took my breath away; how glorious to ride the wind like that, as if the air was solid to him, like waves of water or hills of scree, the tiny bits of rock that cover a mountain side. He was off to the forest now; I knew where one of his nests was hidden. He was probably going hunting for lunch.

I wished my eyes were as sharp as his—Grandfather said that an eagle's eye is almost the same size as mine, but he can see more than 4 to 5 times farther than any human.[1] I was going to practice being "eagle-eyed" now and back in New York.

41

Lunch stew sounded good; I was hungry. It was awkward and a little painful getting to my feet without bending my knee, but I did it. I took one last, sweeping look at my domain. Then I saw it. At first, I thought it just a rock, a lichen-covered piece of granite. But granite doesn't move!

---

1. "Eagles have 20/4 and 20/5 vision while humans have up [to] 20/20 vision. Even though eagles weigh around 10 lbs, eagle's eyes are the same size as humans. Their vision is so precise that they can spot a rabbit up to 3.2km away" (https://chipper-birds.com/facts-about-eagles/).

CHAPTER 10

$\mathcal{N}$ew York City

RUTH HURRIED down the stairs and past the dining room, already wearing her coat and clutching her purse; the smell of breakfast nauseated her. Mrs. Shaw intercepted her dash for the door.

"Ruth," her voice kind but stern, "You cannot keep skipping meals; we haven't seen you for breakfast in weeks. You've paid for them as part of your rent; this is a boarding house, remember?"[1] When Ruth's eyes filled with tears, Mrs. Shaw continued in a gentler tone. "You must eat, dear, or you'll fall ill, and we can't care for you here. You know that." She handed her a waxed paper package. "I've asked Cook to make you a meal to eat on the streetcar. Promise me you will."

"You are too kind, Mrs. Shaw." Ruth sniffed as she regained her composure. "I will eat it; I promise. I don't wish to become ill or be a burden, but I've no appetite at all."

Mrs. Shaw nodded. "I will see you at dinner this evening, Ruth. No excuses, my dear, none at all." Ruth nodded and left, clutching the bundle of food.

"Poor girl," murmured Mrs. Shaw. "Poor, poor girl. I think that

43

those *Missing in Action* telegrams are even more devastating than the *Death* grams. How do you even begin to mourn what is unknown?"

True to her word, Ruth slowly ate the food from Cook. It was kindness that motivated Mrs. Shaw, and the desire to keep her home full of healthy boarders. The food was tasteless to Ruth, dry and unappetizing as bones. When she exited the streetcar and threw away the wrappings, she could not have said what she'd just eaten for breakfast.

After changing into her work overalls, Ruth waited with the other women for the shift change. What would she do without this job to occupy her fingers and distract her brain, she wondered?

Although she committed her full concentration to the task, knowing the importance of ammunition to the war effort, Tom Timothy's face kept floating across her vision. Her dear boy, those eyes of curiosity and wonder! How quickly he'd mastered words, a brilliant mind, like his father's! But his lip—oh, how he suffered from that lip. She'd tried to protect him, shelter him in the house, but he'd still suffered from the cruelty, not always deliberate, of others. Stares, whispers, and pointed fingers—her poor boy! Sometimes he was so withdrawn into himself that she feared for him and his future.

Hopefully, his grandfather was kind. Tom had never mentioned that his father was cruel, no, just rigid in his religion. She'd never have sent her boy to a cruel man.

Tom Timothy's letters were always happy, but he never mentioned many people, just his grandfather and a woman named Miss Rachel. Perhaps he was safer there, with its smaller population and the isolation of the farm. She believed that he was safe, but from his letters, she sometimes worried that he might be bored without the excitement of the city.

But school? He'd hated school here in New York, except when he was with Gio. His grades were always good, but he stayed home whenever she would permit him, and he never wanted to attend any functions, not even the Spelling Bee, which he could probably have won. He never told her of any incidents, but his bright blue eyes always dimmed when she mentioned school, so she stopped questioning him. Hopefully, the smaller Maine schoolhouse would be better for him.

44

She stopped sorting the bullets, her hands falling to her lap. Had she done the right thing? Once she left the apartment and moved into the boarding house, she had forced her own hand. There was no going back! There was no longer a home for Tom Timothy in Brooklyn.

"Miss Ruth, Miss Ruth!" The hand roughly shaking her shoulder and the whispered urgency of the foreman's voice brought her back to her surroundings. "Are you well? Do you need a break? You're falling behind, you know."

"I'm sorry, sir, so sorry. I don't know what happened. I'm fine now." Her fingers flew as she sorted the bullets, desperate to keep her job. "Just fine, really, sir." She breathed easier once he walked away.

The women seated beside her at the long table felt her anxiety—they too knew the need to keep this job as well as the looming uncertainty that threatened everyone who had a husband, son, brother, or lover in the war. Most days, an atmosphere of insecurity permeated the entire warehouse.

Ruth was more exhausted than usual when her shift ended that evening. She had spent all her will and power of concentration to dismiss the images of Tom and Tom Timothy that kept trying to enter her mind. More than once, she had to stop for a few seconds to squeeze her hands tightly, letting her nails dig into the skin, forcing the thoughts away.

The streetcar was crowded that evening, but none of her fellow travelers registered in her consciousness. Now she was free to think about her loved ones, to allow their faces and all the memories to envelop her. In her thoughts, the little apartment was always filled with laughter, Tom Timothy had no worries, and Tom danced with her, humming "Don't Sit Under the Apple Tree" in her ear, then making Tom Timothy laugh as he belted out 'Swinging on a Star." For a moment, all her worries left her, and her depression lifted. So consumed with the happy memories, Ruth nearly missed her stop.

"Oh, dear," she reminded herself, "I must change for dinner now. I must." Trying to keep alive the joy and peace of her thoughts from the ride home, Ruth washed and dressed in a distracted state. She was still a bit dazed when she entered the dining room. Mrs. Shaw was pleased and smiled slightly to see Ruth take her seat at the table. There was even a little bit of color in the poor girl's cheeks. Perhaps she was finally coming to terms with her loss, thought Mrs. Shaw with approval.

---

1. "Many townsfolk dwelled in domiciles in which paying guests are provided with meals and lodging. The accommodations usually consisted of one room per renter or family, while the food was often eaten with other guests at a common table served by the owner" (https://www.jaxhistory.org/portfolio-items/boarding-houses-2/).

   "Shared meals and common areas facilitated the feeling of home in a large family, and proprietors often were charged with maintaining a certain standard of morality for those coming under their care" (https://www.theamericanconserva-tive.com/urbs/the-boarding-houses-that-built-america/).

CHAPTER 11

 ermany

WHEN TOM REGAINED CONSCIOUSNESS, he lay still, listening for the constant noise of his fellow soldiers in the barracks, their laughter and curses. He hesitated to open his eyes, willing himself to see men playing cards, smoking cigarettes, reading letters. Surely this nightmare was over, and he would wake in his bunk, safe in the barracks or at least in an Allied hospital. But his spirits sank as his aching body felt the cold of a packed, dirt floor. Opening his eyes to the dreaded blackness, he knew something was different from the last time he was awake, and his defensive senses went on full alert. He could see nothing in the dark, and it still smelled and sounded like a barn with cows. Nevertheless, something had changed, he was certain. Yet it was so dark, he feared to move. Tom lay rigid, straining to hear and see.

Holding his breath, he waited, but there were no stomping boots or shouts in German. Except for the occasional snort or stamp of an animal, it was as dark and void of light and sound as a tomb. Tom was alone.

Slowly and silently, he moved his left hand to his chest. His fingers felt like ice against his warm chest. Warm? Why did that temperature contrast startle him? He had been so cold, but now? He felt carefully. There were two blankets covering him! Was he losing his mind? Surely he could differentiate between one and two blankets! In what prison did they ever care if a prisoner was freezing? Yes, a second woolen blanket now covered him, and he no longer shook with cold. But now he started to shake with panic, as he feared his reason was leaving him.

He forced himself to lay still and breathe slowly, to remember the cell and his position from earlier in the day. Only one blanket had been there; he would swear to it. He lay silent and motionless, trying again to hear anything that wasn't a cow, but he soon reassured himself that he was still alone. He wanted to sit up, but not until the faintness and nausea left him.

He tentatively began to feel the space around him—the Bible was still there. Still only one, he tried to joke with himself. He remembered the Bible from earlier, but now there was something else, something extra. Another blanket? he marveled. No, it was a small cloth. His fingers kept feeling. No, not a cloth or a blanket, but a shirt! He felt sleeves! A shirt! It was of a rough homespun material but smelled clean. What was happening here? If he was losing his mind, at least it was a pleasant delusion.

Extra blankets, clean clothes—was he in an underground hotel? Sarcasm, mixed with fear and fever, nearly pushed him into delirium. His breath was shallow, gasping, and his right hand clutched the blankets to his chest. *Stop!* he commanded himself. *I must stay in control of my body and mind if I am to survive the elements and my fevered imagination. I cannot succumb to sickness or fear. I will not allow madness to take me. I will not. I will not!* He muttered the command over and over until his breathing returned to normal.

Then he pushed himself up to a sitting position. *Enough with the imagining, Tom, it's time to check out what's wrong with this arm,* he whispered. He grunted with pain as his fingers clumsily bumped a deep and crusted laceration. *Ouch, that was real enough,* he thought. He wondered how he would keep the wound clean; wouldn't it be ironic

48

to survive a plane crash into enemy territory and then die of an infected cut! Sweet Ruth would tell him to stop the gallows humor, after she finished laughing. Ruth—he'd have to clean the cut somehow if he was going to get home to her.

He reached over his left side to continue his tactile investigation; his son would like that description. "Tactile, Father, using only your fingers to explore and learn, tactile!" A wave of emotion swept over him as imagined his son's response. He shuddered and tried to control himself.

He continued the search and was surprised when his fingers felt a compact canvas bag. He gasped, then ran his fingers along the zipper. It was the correct dimensions, the right weight and shape.[1] No, it couldn't be—there had been no first aid kit in his cell last night! And it felt as full as when he'd attached it to ring of his jacket before climbing in the cockpit. This was impossible!

He could hear his father now, a deep voice invading his fevered thoughts. "No, Thomas, not impossible, but a miracle. The Hand of God, my boy, has never left you." Tom made the mistake of shaking his head in denial, and the concussed tissues rebelled. *Oh*, he groaned and covered his eyes with his shaking hand.

He knew that he was feverish, and he feared that the delusions were taking over his rational mind. He needed water; clean water was essential. But he'd finished that jug earlier, if it had ever even existed. He thought back; water, water and food had been at his feet. He fought the urge to pray, thrusting it from his mind. He reached a shaking hand toward his feet. Nothing. Nothing lay at his feet.

He remembered a line from Psalms that mocked him now: "Thou madest him to have dominion over the works of thy hands; thou hast put all things under his feet."[2] *Not all things, God, not all things, just some water!* he prayed in desperation, and his right hand swept wide. He jerked back as his fingers brushed against the coarse cloth. *Please be real*, he whispered and leaned forward. His hand gently explored, feeling its dimensions. He could see nothing. Taking a deep breath, he reached under the fabric, and his fingers trembled against the cool ceramic jug and the crusty bread. He started to weep silently.

---

1. "The canvas rectangular case closed with a zipper (when completely opened, it allowed to unfold the container) and seal bearing the proper MD identification and consisted of two separate large compartments, with a smaller separate pouch closing with a press stud, while the outside envelope also contained some limited medical items...MAIN KIT: 1 Tube, Burn Injury Set, Boric Ointment; 1 Eye Dressing Set; 2 Morphine Tartrate, Tubes; 1 Box, Sulfadiazine, 12 Tablets; 1 Envelope, Sulfanilamide, Crystalline; 3 Dressings, First-Aid, Small, White; 1 Scissors, 4-Inch, Straight, 1 Point Sharp; 1 Tourniquet, Field, with Pad; OUTSIDE ENVELOPE OF KIT: 1 Box, Iodine Swab, 10-Minim, 10; 1 Box, Bandage, Gauze, Adhesive, 1-Inch x 3-Inch, 16; 1 Bottle, Halazone Tablets, 100" (https://www.med-dept.com/medical-kits-contents/kits-of-military-aircraft/).
2. Psalm 8:6 KJV - "Thou madest him to have dominion over the works of thy hands; thou hast put all things under his feet."

CHAPTER 12

 ermany

AFTER EATING AND DRINKING, Tom fell once again into a deep sleep. He awoke to the sounds of day, it seemed a late and dim daylight, and the same nightmare. But there were a few more gifts in his cell.

Today there was even fresh straw, a chamber pot, clean rags, and a bowl of water at the end of his blankets, in addition to a very welcome pair of worn woolen pants, too big at the waist and too short in the legs. *Either I've got a fairy godmother, or someone is drugging my water and coming in here while I'm passed out*, he reasoned. *But I'm not complaining; I'm just confused*, he hastened to assure himself.

The chamber pot[1] had his immediate attention. And then he used the clean water and bandages with the supplies from the first aid kit to clean up his left arm. He needed stitches, but that was beyond his ability today; just cleaning it was enough. After his ablutions—that's what his boy called washing up in the mornings—Tom sat back exhausted and looked around.

He heard boots above him, but they weren't stomping and seemed to belong to a single person; the deep lowing of a couple of cows was clearly both a greeting and a request to the farmer. The animals were not afraid, Tom was sure. The cows did that at home, he remembered, when they were hungry and ready to be milked. Although the cows were calm, he knew that they were in a safer environment than he was; until he met his fairy godmother, he would consider this a prison cell in hostile territory.

What was going on? Was he in an experiment? He'd been briefed back at flight school about different types of torture, and they'd even mentioned psychological warfare. Was that what was happening to him? Were they trying to change his loyalties, to break his will to fight, by tricking him? Would they feed and clothe him, make him grateful to them and totally dependent on them, and then demand information about his flights and America's war plans? He needed to stay sharp; he couldn't let them make him feel comfortable and complacent. This was war! They didn't know how he had been raised, with loyalty to God, country, and family, and he still believed in America and would die defending his home and his family. They couldn't turn him!

Tom rubbed his face hard, trying to make himself fully alert. Rough stubble fully covered his chin and cheeks. How long had he been down here? His sense of time had been twisted by the concussion and further distorted by the dark conditions of the cell. His training taught him to take control over his circumstances, as much as he could. Yes, keep a calendar, rebuild his strength, discover the true nature of his captors, find possible ways to escape them, pinpoint his location and then plan an escape route. Yes, take control now. That would keep him sane! Sane and ready to fight back!

He had to stand now, get himself strong again and ready for combat, or at least for escape. His head bumped the floor above before he realized the cell dimensions—about 7 feet long and less than 5 feet high. He was trapped in a little box!

He fought back the panic and forced himself to think logically. He was incarcerated by unknown forces, almost certainly the Nazis, but he was being treated humanely. He had water and some food, clothes and blankets to keep him from freezing to death. It could be worse, much worse. His father would have said for him to be thankful, but that was absurd. Why should he be thankful for crashing in the depths of Germany and being captured as a prisoner of war! Thankful? No, he was angry. Anger would serve him much better than gratitude.

Anger and his father—they were linked together in his mind and spirit. It had been so many years since he'd thought of his father without a flood of anger and resentment. It was probably good, that connection. Anger would fuel his escape; thoughts of his father would be good for something now. But not guilt, he quickly drove that feeling away from his mind.

Trying to stand and making tentative plans had tired him, and the deep fatigue worried him. He didn't have time to rest; he had to prepare. He carefully moved his left arm, assuring himself that the pain had lessened a bit. He rested his head against the earthen wall and breathed deeply. No sleeping now.

He hadn't noticed it initially, but in the dim, filtered light, he could still see that something else had changed. He thought for a moment, and then it was obvious—how had he missed it. It was that Bible. It was open! He certainly hadn't touched it. He shook his head at the strangeness of the event and was about to close it when he noticed a discoloration, a marking of some sort on the page. He shifted his position, scooting across the floor until one of the slivers of light through the floorboards shone down upon the book.

The pages were so thin, almost translucent, and they fluttered slightly as he lifted it to the light. He hadn't picked up a Bible in over fifteen years, and he'd never opened this one, just carried it with him

53

always, in keeping with his promise to Ruth when he left the States. He looked closely at the open pages in the thin beam of illumination; the narrow sunbeam shone clearly, highlighting the page like a flashlight. He'd been right. There was a marking—why would anyone deface his book? He looked more closely.

It was the book of John, chapter 14, and verse 27^2 that was marked. Charcoal or a very stubby pencil had circled the first word. Breathing deeply, Tom put the book down cautiously, as far away as he could in the tiny cell, as though it might detonate if he weren't extremely careful.

---

1. A pot or vessel used as an indoor toilet.
2. "Peace I leave with you, my peace I give unto you: not as the world giveth, give I unto you. Let not your heart be troubled, neither let it be afraid" (KJV).

CHAPTER 13

$\mathcal{M}$aine

August 18, 1943

Now I had another dilemma, a true predicament. There was something on the shore that I'd never seen, that I must investigate, but I was supposed to rest my knee. I should go get Grandfather; he could help me down the rocky path. But by the time I limped over to him and found him in the cornfield, if he was even still there, it might be gone!

It would be irresponsible to allow this mystery to escape. War correspondents have to take chances, risk danger to find the truth. How would I be able to sleep tonight if I let it get away? Gio would be so disappointed in me too.

Taking a second look at the path down, it didn't look so steep. There were a few small firs and birches that I could grab to steady myself, but it would be slow going. I'm sure Grandfather'll understand. He was a boy once too.

But what was down there? It was pretty big and definitely alive, rocks don't move! I wondered if it was dangerous. I'd never thought a moose could be so violent; I thought it would just be a big deer, sweet like the deer in that movie Bambi. I saw the movie just last year—it was a treat for Mother and me, one we'd saved our money for since Christmas. I knew it was for little kids, but we liked it anyway. Now Bambi wasn't real, not like the moose, not

55

like the war. I needed to be careful now, not just with walking but with investigating, too.

By grabbing the branches of the firs and birches on my way down, I slowed my descent and kept control of my feet. There were a couple of close calls, but I finally made it. I decided that while it might take me a bit longer, I was definitely going to the boathouse to get that clam rake—those sharp teeth could protect me from most creatures. I was going to be prepared! Not a moose; I knew that was no moose down on the shore. But what could it be? I'd read a few books about sea creatures, and I was pretty sure that neither a squid nor an octopus could lay camouflaged on the rocky shore. I was glad that sharks and whales were confined to the water. I wondered.

I made it! The beach always felt so good to walk on, sand and little bits of gravel and sea-smoothed shell pieces. I never walked barefoot in Brooklyn—I would miss this beach!

It sure was different down here: the rocks sighed louder, and the waves crashed more. The sea gulls were screeching their welcome cries. Now I needed to situate myself and find that moving rock. I went slowly, sliding my feet through the sand, keeping the rake in front of me. I was ready for anything!

I was surprised I saw it, half-hidden by yellow rockweed, still and silent. The hunched grey body, tucked among the rocks, reminded me of the boulders thrown by a blinded giant[1]. Only its eyes moved, blinking in surprise and fear. I froze too. I probably noticed it because of the blood—it was hurt! It needed help: I knew it needed me. As I moved closer, it hissed and snapped its jaws. Teeth, I saw so many sharp teeth! I stumbled backwards, away from its wildness. I fell on the sand, narrowly missing the points of the clamming rake. My heart pounded and my knee throbbed as I scrambled back, fearing its attack, but it didn't move. It hadn't moved anything but its head.

I needed Grandfather—this was beyond my abilities. I'd learned a lot this summer, but I had no idea how to handle this situation. I left the clam rake and hurried as fast as my limping gait would let me. This was an emergency!

When you couldn't bend your knee, going up was a lot harder than going down. I didn't think about that when I first saw the moving rock. But I was not going to bust open those stitches by bending my knee, no way. Why I even went up backwards, butt first, in the steepest areas.

I was sweating by the time I got back up to the top of the bluff. I could move much faster on the grassy meadow, but I had quite a ways to go to the cornfields. I started yelling for Grandfather once I got close to the house, but he wasn't there. I hurried toward the fields, calling out every time I needed to stop to catch my breath, but there was no response.

Finally, I heard him, "Boyo?" His deep voice carried through the stalks of corn that towered over my head. "Boyo?"

"Here I am," I shouted, "here I am." I heard the corn stalks rustling before I saw him. He pushed the thick green plants aside as he hurried down the row. I could see the concern in his face and his hurried glance toward my knee.

"What is it, Tom Timothy? You're supposed to be resting that knee." The corn stalks stood taller than Grandfather, keeping us both in the shadows.

"I'm okay, Grandfather, but there's an emergency, a crisis down on the shore! There was blood, and I tried to help, but it tried to attack me!"

"On the shore? Blood? I'm confused, Boyo! What were you doing down on the shore? I thought you were resting on the top. And what's bleeding and attacking?"

"Grandfather!" I pulled on his arm and turned back to the shore, "Come now! It's a crisis. I couldn't handle it myself, I tried! I need you, Grandfather, I need you now!"

He began to shake his head but then nodded with a slight smile. "All right. You start back, Tom Timothy. First, I've got to unsaddle Balaam and move him to a shady, grassy spot in case we are gone for a bit. Be careful, but start walking. I'll catch up with you. By the way, do you think I'll need my gun?"

His gun! "Of course, Grandfather, we must be prepared for anything!" I shouted over my shoulder as I limped away quickly.

---

1. As allusion to Homer's *Odyssey* when the Cyclops threw boulders at Odysseus trying to escape.

57

CHAPTER 14

$\mathcal{M}$aine

I WASN'T EVEN BACK to the house before Grandfather was beside me. He slowed his pace to match mine.

"Well, Boyo, now how about some more information about this crisis, this emergency of yours? It must be something very extreme, maybe even dangerous, to make you work that knee so hard."

Now, why did he have to mention my knee? Once he did, it started hurting again. I slowed my pace even more. But I was still a journalist, wasn't I? I had to keep my readers reading, had to keep a bit of mystery in the story, so I answered him thoughtfully. "Grandfather, I think it would be best if you got your gun, your thick leather gloves, and any other protection you can think of. You need to see it with your own eyes, but let's hurry. High tide will be here in a couple of hours."

He just looked at me quizzically and grunted an assent, but he didn't move. Grandfather shifted his eyes back toward the fields of corn and rubbed his chin in thought.

"Grandfather, time is of the essence, as Sherlock would say, or he should have said! Why don't you stop here at the house and pick up the supplies and weapons while I head to the bluff? I'll wait for you at the top." He finally nodded, and I sighed in relief.

I didn't need to tell him that I probably wouldn't be able to make it down without him anyway. Weapons—his gun—that was much better than a clam rake! I couldn't wait to tell Gio!

I reached the bluff before Grandfather and peered intently over the edge. Now that I knew what I was looking for, I found it quickly. I could even see the blood this time—it wasn't lichen, rockweed, kelp, or even early autumn leaves; it was blood. When Grandfather finally got there, his arms were full. He carried his gun in his right hand while his left hand secured a large burlap bag that he'd swung over his left shoulder. I hoped he'd remembered lots of bullets, just in case. Maybe he brought more guns!

He set down the bag and leaned over the edge. "All right, Tom Timothy, I'm here with the gear you suggested and then some. Just where are we looking?"

I felt like an explorer, like Lewis and Clark, like Columbus![1] I'd found it; I'd discovered it, all by myself! I pointed down. "See the four boulders, right up against the bluff?" He nodded silently, his eyes following my finger. "Well, they aren't all boulders. One of them is alive! And bloody. Look carefully, Grandfather. Do you see?"

He looked for a moment, then straightened to his full height and cleared his throat. "Yep, something's hurt down there for sure. Did you say you'd been down to the beach already? With that knee? Why didn't you just come and get me immediately?"

"I went slowly, Grandfather, very carefully. I used the birch branches and fir limbs to help keep steady and in control. My knee's okay, really. I didn't want to come and get you until I was sure it was something, something alive. I didn't notice any blood the first time I looked."

"Injured creatures can be dangerous, Tom Timothy, very dangerous. They are in pain and afraid. That makes them aggressive. Don't you remember the moose?"

Would I ever forget that moose? "Don't worry, Grandfather, I was smart and careful. Why, I took time to go to the boathouse and get the clam rake for defense. See, it's there in front of the rock! I was ready for anything."

He carefully leaned his gun against the nearby maple and then put his hands on my shoulders. "Boyo, I need to teach you so much more. There is

59

wildness in these woods and waters. I'm sorry I've been so busy with the farm; winter is a better time for instruction."

"It's okay, Grandfather. You can hurry and teach me a lot before I leave. I'm a quick learner! Now let's go down to the shore before the tide shuts us out."

"All right, but you wait here a moment. I'm going to take down this bag and the gun first. I want both hands free to help you on the descent. It looks like you nearly pulled up a sapling or two on your previous trip down. I'll replant them tomorrow; erosion will wear this cliff away if we don't take care."

He was right; I'd hoped he wouldn't notice, but Grandfather seemed to have the eyes of an eagle at times. Waiting was the least I could do—he'd left his crops and his horse for me. I tried to wait patiently for him to go down and then come back up again.

Going down with Grandfather was swifter than before. He had a tight grip on my right arm and steadied me when I started to slip. He even lifted me over the large rocks that I'd awkwardly crawled over before. Nevertheless, I breathed a sigh of relief when my feet met the sandy beach. We'd made it. Grandfather retrieved his gun and the bag and motioned for me to lead the way.

I quickly reached my marker—the clam hoe on the beach. Grandfather frowned; "Never leave a hoe or rake pointing up, Boyo. It's a danger!"

"Yes, sir," I replied, and I quickly flipped it over, burying its sharp teeth in the gravel. I wouldn't need it now; Grandfather had his gun!

"There, Grandfather, look! It's not a rock, and it's hurt!"

Grandfather took only a step or two forward and stopped, shaking his

60

head. I kept close to him, but just a little bit behind. I remembered my previous greeting as an uncomfortable brush of fear slid down my spine. Grandfather set the bag on a flat rock but kept his gun; he didn't go any closer. Then he put up his hand to shade his eyes, squatted down, and looked quietly for a moment. I kept my hand on his back.

"Poor old seal," he finally said softly. "Who's gone and hurt you, huh?"

---

1. Lewis and Clark were famous American explorers sent by President Jefferson in 1804 to explore the land west of the Mississippi River as well as the Northwest region of the country.

CHAPTER 15

$\mathcal{M}$aine

"WHAT HAPPENED, Grandfather, what do you think happened? Can we help it? I think it is scared and hurt. It's got a lot of teeth and snapped at me earlier, so be careful. Be careful, Grandfather." I couldn't seem to stop talking. "See the blood there? What happened, a shark or a whale or what?"

"I'll be careful, and you remember, seals can carry a lot of disease, so do not touch them, dead or alive. Do you understand?" When I nodded, he put his hand on my shoulder, either to keep me quiet or to help him slowly rise to his feet. "Not a shark, Tom Timothy, nothing out of the ocean hurt this poor seal." His eyes flashed with anger as he gripped my shoulder tightly for an instance, and I felt his fury. Then it all seemed to fade, as though a wave of tiredness, deep fatigue, swept over him, and he shoved his hands into his pockets. "No, Boyo, it wasn't God's nature that wounded this poor creature, it was human nature. Some fool shot it." He spit with disgust onto the graveled beach.

"Shot it, are you sure?" My head spun around as I scanned the waters and bluff for snipers. "Is your gun loaded and ready, Grandfather?"

His voice was softer now as he answered me. "I don't think this poor

62

fellow will be attacking us, Tom Timothy. And whoever shot him probably did it yesterday. It's not likely you'll ever have such a chance as this, so look closely—his hide is torn up from shot gun spray. He must have been diving when someone pulled the trigger."

I felt braver with Grandfather beside me, so I stepped closer to look. Grandfather surprised me by handing me my journal and pen out of the bag he brought. "I thought this adventure might need documenting, Boyo." He was right; a journalist needed to be prepared and always take notes.

I studied the creature, and Grandfather answered some questions for me.

"He looks to be about 5 feet long and close to 250 pounds—he's a big, full-grown seal." I nodded my agreement and started writing.

His round black eyes are almost human, filled with pain, fear, and exhaustion; they remind me of Gio's after we got beat up in the alley. The seal's chin is whiskered, grey liked Grandfather's but not a beard, just thick whiskers jutting out to the sides and up over his eyes like crazy eyebrows. His head looks a bit like a person's, but he has no ears, so I guess those verses from Grandfather's Bible don't apply to him.[1] His mouth is closed, and the snout looks a bit like a dog—a short muzzle and black, wet nose. And I remember the teeth he showed, definitely sharp, pointy, and numerous. Now that I'm closer, I can see his fur, camouflaged to match the lichen spotted granite rocks. I thought he looked shiny and slick at first, but it isn't wet, just thick, short fur, thicker than any dog I've ever seen. And no arms or legs, just flippers that look useless to it now and a short stub of a tail that is almost finned. It looks powerful but helpless. I know it is hurt, but even so, its strength doesn't promise much on land.

Grandfather stood quietly while I wrote furiously. When I set down my pen and looked up, he said, "Lots of folks don't understand the brilliance of the Creator. This animal that looks so clumsy and awkward on the beach is a picture of grace and beauty as it swims the seas; it can dive and twist, leap and play in the water with an elegance and speed we humans can only dream of."

I nodded, wondering how he knew so many of my thoughts and questions before I even spoke.

"It's strong and beautiful and funny-looking, all at the same time, Grandfather."

"Aren't we all, Boyo? Aren't we all?" He shook his head and pointed back at the seal. "Do you see where the pellets tore into its body? See the thick white layers? That's the fat of the seal. It coats his body, under his fur, and keeps him warm in the iciest of waters and winters. Isn't it marvelous?"

"Yes, Grandfather," but I had to stop this train of thought before we were back to his Bible and his God. "But he's hurt. Shouldn't we go get Miss Rachel? Couldn't she help him?" I figured a big poultice might ease some of its suffering.

"No, Tom Timothy, no. Miss Rachel couldn't help this poor wild creature, and she'd be so upset to see it. She's a kind woman who feels deeply the pain of others—she is a woman of compassion. And it saddens her when she can't help."

"But we have to do something! We can't just walk away and leave it bleeding and dying on the beach." An image of my father, hurt and dying appeared in my mind. "We have to do something; we can't just leave it, all alone!" I shouted and banged my fists against my thighs to drive the thought away.

"Easy, Tom Timothy," Grandfather said as he moved us back away from the seal who had lifted its head in alarm. "Seals hear well, better than they see, and you don't want to scare him anymore than he already is." He walked me over to a pile of boulders that were still dry from the tide.

"I'm sorry, Boyo, but we can't help him other than to toss some minnows and small fish his way. Miss Rachel does not have medicine to heal a creature from the sea, only the salt water itself can help him. I'm thinking he beached himself, dragged himself onto high dry ground, to rest safely. As people of the earth with limited knowledge of the sea, the only thing we can do is pray to Almighty God for the seal."

"Pray, Grandfather, pray? I don't understand. Why did your God let him get shot in the first place? Why?" I felt angry and so sad at the same time.

---

1. Matthew 11:15 "He that hath ears to hear, let him hear" (KJV).

64

CHAPTER 16

$\mathcal{U}$niversity of Maine – 1930s

RUTH WAS NOT a weak woman nor a timid soul. Her strength and vitality had been a strong attraction for Tom and for most people who met her. Not needy, but rather a giver, she shared her strength and fresh optimism with others. In college, her housemates sought refuge in her when broken hearts and disappointments threatened. She talked more than one friend away from self-doubt and crippling despair. Even the Dean of Women had referred at least one weepy co-ed to Ruth's care.

Millicent's pale blue eyes were red-rimmed and shadowed. She'd been crying all night rather than resting. As part of the minority of female students on the U Maine campus, she'd initially basked in the initial attention of dozens of possible beaus. Now, she wept; she knew she'd made a mistake in choosing to date Bradley exclusively—his selfishness and self-absorption were now visible through his blue-eyed façade of chivalry. The small man thought he was dapper and charming, but Ruth had immediately seen him as an insecure manipulator. His compliments to Millie were always loaded. "Well, you look beautiful today, Honey, keep it up!" How is today any different from yesterday, Milly wondered more than once. The pretty girl loved his compliments, but they unseated her confidence. His words often made her doubt herself but never led her to question him.

Ruth couldn't understand the attraction; she'd seen him as a little bully from the beginning, a man who only smiled with his mouth.

"What do I do, Ruth? I thought he was the one!" Millie wailed. A bit dramatic, thought Ruth, but Millie was a member of the theater club.

"I'm so sorry, Milly, but you have a lot to be happy about—you're beautiful, smart, and safe!"

"Safe?" sniffled the girl, wiping her eyes with a lace hanky. "What do you mean, safe?"

"I mean, you've seen his true character <u>before</u> you married him. Girl, as my Momma always said, 'Men's weaknesses only get worse once that honeymoon has set!' You need to move on. Find a man who's honest and true rather than slick. Really, Millie, believe in yourself and end it with Bradley, and you'll see a group of better men at your door before you know it."

But in her situation, none of her girlfriends offered any opinions or advice about Tom other than how handsome and kind he was, so she had to interrogate herself, forcing truth to shine even in the haze of her first love. Popular on campus with his deep laugh and quick wit, Tom was certainly considered a catch, but Ruth was wary. He spoke so little about his home and was clearly estranged from his father, a relationship he quietly but steadfastly refused to discuss.

Ruth worried because she wanted a home. She had been aching for a family and its comforts since 1926, when *The Ponce de Leon* train struck the *Royal Palm* and left her a teenaged orphan. As an only child, the sudden loss of her parents left Ruth alone, devastated and bewildered. She knew of no relatives and was grateful to stay with the local minister and his wife until she graduated high school. The kind, elderly couple had shared their home and faith, and Ruth would always think of them with thankfulness, but her questions needed more of an explanation than their repeated murmurs of "God's will."

Armed with a small inheritance and two traveling trunks, she left her hometown in northern Georgia with its happy memories of her youth as well as the fears and depression of her lonely adolescence. She wanted to go as far north as she could go, hoping to escape the popular country song that told and retold her loss with a Southern twang. "The Wreck of the Royal Palm Express"[1] seemed to celebrate her loss, plunging her back into darkness. Forcing herself to board the northbound train, she fiercely gripped the seat and closed her eyes against thoughts of her parents' last trip. After a day, her exhausted muscles and weary mind gave up, and she began to enjoy the new vistas. Her imagination peopled the towns and named the livestock along the tracks. Ruth's journey ended at Maine's outpost university, in the northern town of Orono, almost to Canada. She joined the Outing Club, suffering through the first year's hikes in the waist-deep snow, and majored in English with a minor in Home Economics. With the dismal economic state of the country, it was not a debatable second choice, but Ruth had never lost her hope for an exciting and fulfilling future. Marriage with Tom, she decided quickly, had been proof of her prescience.

After a quick but intense courtship, they joined their lives in a quiet wedding. Neither of them trusted time nor circumstance—there were too many unknowns in their worlds. Ruth wanted to continue with her studies even though many in the world of academia frowned on married women in college, especially those who considered a wedding ring the only true goal of a woman's enrollment in higher education. Tom and Ruth moved off campus into a cheap and cramped apartment, old and drafty, but just a short walk to classes. The Depression still hovered around them, a blight on both the beautiful northern town and the prospects of the hopeful and energetic students. Money was tight, but they felt rich in their love for one another. Tom loved her cooking and nurturing nature. "Ruthie, I'm so glad I never have to iron another shirt. You're better at it than I ever could be, and you even look beautiful doing it!" His eyes twinkled as he embraced her, carefully avoiding the scorching heat of the iron.

"Well, Tom, I didn't come to college to become anyone's wife or scullery maid," she pulled away from his arms, "but I do love caring for you. Living with you. Loving you." She kissed him quickly, then continued her work on his shirt. "Besides, I've already got you." She smiled at him, handing him the freshly ironed shirt. He was expected to show up for classes in a suit and tie, if not in his military attire.

Like all physically fit males in the freshmen class, Tom had participated in the state required two-year military training course. Due to his natural agility, strength ("moving boulders and hauling in the crops is better than any weight set"), and innate competitiveness, Tom was among the twenty men offered an advanced military training course because he knew that the rank of Second Lieutenant in the Reserves might enable him to someday fly the Mustang, the only position he desired for himself, if it came to war. Ruth hated talk of the war, but like Tom, she loved her country, a place that had welcomed her great grandparents from Eastern Europe, so she tried never to show Tom her fears. And she knew his reasoning was right: "I'd rather go in as an officer, hon, than a grunt." She rested in her knowledge of their love. They both feared they were living on borrowed time, but it did little to quench their joy.

Tom was thrilled when she met him at the door with champagne, an extravagance on their limited budget. She watched his face closely as it progressed from confusion to possibility to delight. "A baby! A baby? We're having a baby?" he finally exclaimed. She wasn't even able to answer him before he smothered her in an embrace, lifting her off the floor in his excitement. He quickly put her down, a bit chagrined, but recovered quickly when she assured him that she was fine, that hugging and lifting were also fine.

They talked late into the night, whispering in intimacy, sharing dreams about their growing family. Ruth's pregnancy was uneventful except for cravings for the jars of dill pickles put up by the farm women outside of town. Tom laughed and kept their little cupboard well stocked. Cuddling at night under two quilts and a woolen blanket, they discussed names for the baby, and she was warmed by the tears that shone in his eyes as he spoke of his late mother and his desire to name the baby after her. Elizabeth was a beautiful name, but they'd call her Lizzie; it was the perfect name for their little one, and certainly if it were a boy, it would be Thomas Junior, insisted Ruth, though her husband seemed hesitant.

68

1. "The Wreck of the Royal Palms Express," recorded just three weeks after the horrible crash. To summarize the lyrics: "On the Royal Palm and Ponce de Leon trains, heading home for Christmas, all is cheerful despite a storm. The trains collide; many are killed or hurt. The singer warns hearers to keep their orders straight; if they get their orders mixed it'll be too late" (http://www.folk-lorist.org/song/Wreck_of_the_Royal_Palm). The original song can be heard on YouTube (https://www.youtube.com › watch?v=Kq_GqaZlBE00).

CHAPTER 17

$\mathcal{U}$niversity of Maine – 1930s

THE BABY WAS due in December, "the best holiday gift ever," Tom told anyone who stopped to listen. The young couple's infectious excitement spread among their friends and neighbors—everyone felt involved and invested in the changes in Tom and Ruth's life. She felt the sharp pains just before daybreak on the last morning before the Christmas break, and Tom skipped classes as he bundled up to trek to the doctor[1], a busy man they'd visited once in downtown Orono. On his way down, Tom knocked on the door of their landlady, apologizing for the early hour but informing her of Ruth's condition and his errand. She assured him she'd check on Ruth as soon as she'd dressed.

Mrs. O'Malley meant well, but her attentions were soon diverted by a stubborn furnace and complaining tenants. There was no heat and no hot water, a bother any time, but truly a nuisance at the start of winter. It was nearly three hours later when Ruth came to Mrs. O'Malley's thoughts, and she hurried up to check on Tom's wife. Having birthed a half dozen children herself, four who had survived,

70

she had no worries about a first child coming too quickly into the world. When Ruth failed to open the door, Mrs. O'Malley let herself in. Finding the young woman so pale, drenched in sweat and meaning, Mrs. O'Malley rushed to the door and shouted for her husband Patrick. She sent him down the street to look for Tom and the doctor.

Tom returned just before Patrick did, and he felt faint as he looked at Ruth. The worry on Mrs. O'Malley's face drove a dagger of fear into his stomach, and he rushed to hold his wife. "I'm here, darling, I'm here. The doctor is on his way up, on his way now," he whispered, stroking her damp forehead, and holding her in his arms.

Inside his mind, he raged with anger, recalling the doctor's lack of interest and procrastination to head out into the snowy cold. *"Well, young sir, I need to shave, dress, and have my breakfast. Very important in such inclement weather. Don't be so impatient. Girls have been giving birth for centuries. Your wife's no different."* When the doctor finally agreed to come to the apartment, Tom rushed to the door. *"Not so fast, young fellow. I must check on a few of my more established customers on the way; finances first, you know."* Tom had been afraid to leave the doctor's car, worried that the man would ultimately decide Ruth wasn't worth the visit. Remembering the man's tone of condescension nearly drove Tom mad as he sat with his weak and suffering wife, but the doctor was downstairs now, slowly walking up the three flights of steep stairs.

Entering the small apartment with Patrick, the doctor crossed the threshold of the room, looking at its occupants for welcome, but he saw only fear. He dropped his coat to the floor and grabbed his medical bag from Patrick then hurried to the girl. "Hot water! Clean towels!" he commanded Mrs. O'Malley. She promptly dispatched Patrick for the towels and rushed to the kitchen—she'd have to fire up that old stove to get any hot water.

Quickly checking her vital signs, the doctor looked at Tom for the first time, compassion then guilt flitted quickly across his face. He rolled up his sleeves and worked intently with Ruth, urging her on, trying to keep the desperation from his voice. After three hours, he looked down on Ruth, nearly as white as the sheets covering her. Tom held a lifeless bundle in his arms, tears dripping down his face as he sobbed silently.

"I'm sorry about the baby," the doctor said quietly, but he backed away quickly from the anger in Tom's eyes. "I did all that anyone could do. Sometimes things go wrong—no one knows why. But I saved your wife. I did, you know."

Tom could not bring himself to speak; he could only stare at the doctor, the man of science, the expert who had failed so miserably. Tom nodded, and the doctor hurried from the cold room, grabbing his coat and bag on the way out. He'd wait to wash until he was in his own warm house.

Mrs. O'Malley tried to take the bundle from Tom, but he wouldn't let go. He shook his head and clutched the baby tighter. "When your wife wakes, she'll want to see the babe. Make it quick, Tom, because the wee one's beauty will cut her to the marrow. I'll wait with you. You can show Ruth, then I'll take her to the church. The Father will take care of her."

Tom wanted to protest, to keep the child from the hands of religion, that false hope that had cheated him first of a mother and now of his daughter, but he was too tired. He dropped his head in acquiescence and waited for Ruth to wake up.

The landlady had spoken with the wisdom of experience. Ruth finally woke, her voice weak and hoarse. One look at her handsome Tom's grief-ravaged face told her everything, but she still reached for the bundle he held close to his chest. "She's a beautiful little girl, Ruthie, but she did not live a moment in this world. She's perfect, but she is gone already," his voice broke and he sobbed loudly as he placed the eternally sleeping infant in her arms.

Ruth stared with wonder at the peaceful face, beautiful but lifeless. She laid her hand against the baby's face, then rested her against her own cheek. The pain that exploded in her heart overwhelmed and silenced the rest of her body as she sobbed and gave the child back to Tom.

After that day, darkness filled Ruth's world, a despair that denied reason and hope. Excitement and anticipation had fled. Only the sight of Tom's loving eyes, the comfort of his strong arms, and his constant whispered promises kept her from the gaping emotional abyss that beckoned her. She knew that only Tom could save her.

---

1. Although more women were giving birth in hospitals, Tom and Ruth's finances made a home birth more affordable. Unlike the choice of a midwife for the home birth, Tom's belief in Science led him to choose a doctor instead.

CHAPTER 18

$\mathcal{M}$aine

August 18, 1943

"God did not shoot that seal, Tom Timothy, but a human did, probably one of the Gagnon boys. They carry an anger and insolence in them that threatens everyone around them. I'll need to pay a visit to their father, to make him aware, but there is little to be expected from him. He drinks a lot and has no time for his sons. They run wild, spreading destruction wherever they go." He shook his head sadly and looked at me.

"Well, won't the law stop them then, Grandfather?"

"Yes, someday, when their hearts are totally hardened and too much damage is done, the law will probably lock them up. Unfortunately, right now, there is no law on the books that prevents shooting seals for sport. The only law that could prevent it is the law that God writes on the hearts of men, a law men can disregard at their own risk."[1]

"If people can disregard God's laws, Grandfather, it doesn't sound like a very good system, does it? John Bunyan[2] wrote about an all-powerful King and you talk about an almighty God; so why doesn't that God do something?" It was hard to talk so harshly to Grandfather, but the words rushed out of me; I couldn't stop them.

74

Grandfather knelt on the rocky shore and looked me in the eye. "Free will, Boyo, free will. It is one of the hardest concepts to understand, as slippery to hold in your mind as to grip water in a fast-flowing stream. Free will is also one of the most precious gifts God has given to his special creation, to humans, only to humans."

I stared into his eyes, blue eyes just like Father's and just like mine, and I saw his pleading. He wanted me to understand so badly. "But what exactly is free will, Grandfather? I understand it is almost incomprehensible yet also valuable, but what is it?"

He smiled slightly. "You already understand more than most people, Boyo." He closed his eyes, as though in silent communication with someone, and then nodded his head. "Free will is the choice, Tom Timothy, to know God or disregard Him, to follow His way or to choose your own path, to accept His love and sacrifice or to reject Him. Free will is our opportunity, our choice to follow the perfect God of the Universe or to make ourselves little gods and tyrants. It is our chance to accept adoption by God and eternal life with Him or to keep our independence and spend eternity without Him. That, Tom Timothy, is just a small glimpse into some of the properties of free will."

"But the poor seal, Grandfather!"

"The seal, like all creatures, is gifted with instincts and natural habits which serve it well. Some animals, like pets, are even gifted with affection and loyalty. But only mankind is blessed with free will. Only mankind is made in the very image of God."

"But what do we do for the seal, Grandfather." The creature seemed to look right into my eyes, and I felt responsible for him because he was my discovery. "What would your God say to do?"

"Well, Boyo, God gave man dominion, which means control and author-ity, over all the earth and its creatures.³ We are supposed to be good stewards, faithful farmers and caretakers, to care for the land, water, and all living things." He stood and stretched slowly. "Now, pick up the clam rake and then let's go to the bait shack and get a couple of buckets and nets. Today, we aren't saltwater farmers but saltwater fisherman, caretakers of that old seal over there."

Before the tide came in and covered the rocks, we'd filled two buckets with minnows of all sizes. Grandfather carefully poured out fish in front of the seal. He hesitated for only a brief moment before he snatched up the

75

minnows, crunching them in his powerful jaws. The second bucketful was eaten just as quickly. We gathered the net and buckets and hurried to the higher part of the bank, where Grandfather had already put the rifle and duffle bag, and we quietly watched the water gently cover[4] the rocky beach and approach the stranded seal.

"The tide's nearly in and the sun's setting, Tom Timothy, we've more chores to do before nightfall. Let's go now." He reached out his hand to help me climb.

I stopped his hand. "Not yet, Grandfather. Why, aren't you going to pray for him?"

He turned and looked at me for a moment and then nodded. He raised his head and lifted his powerful hands toward heaven and poured out words of praise and thanks to his God. Some of the words I couldn't understand, but I could feel the intense passion in them. Then he dropped to his knees. "Almighty God and loving Father, I kneel on this beach and ask your healing touch on the wounded creature on the shore. Please heal its body and give it strength to swim the seas to the glory of your name. Thank you, Lord. Amen and amen." Then he stood and put his arm around my shoulders, and we watched the incoming tide.

The tide kept inching forward, but the seal ignored it; he seemed to have lost all will to live. The water lapped against his snout, but still the seal stared into oblivion, ignoring his ocean home. Salty water crept to its neck, but his eyes showed no reaction. My eyes were filling with tears; it was so sad. Then the waves touched his flippers, and something amazing happened. He lifted his head and inhaled the savory brine. I blinked my eyes and rubbed away the tears. He flexed his flippers and inched forward. When the incoming tide combined with his futile fin-flapping, and when his stubby tail suddenly touched the water, then he surged forward. I was stunned at his quick movements and sudden dive. It was only seconds until he surfaced 15 yards out, then another dive and another 20 yards re-surfacing, with only a brief backward glance.

I looked to Grandfather, and we both laughed with joy as the seal, its wake trailing its underwater movements, swam into a sea of golden sunset.

76

1. Grandfather may be referring to Romans 2:15—They [Gentiles = unbelievers] show that the requirements of the law are written on their hearts, their consciences also bearing witness, and their thoughts sometimes accusing them and at other times even defending them) (NIV).
2. John Bunyan wrote *The Pilgrim's Progress*, a famous Christian allegory. Grandfather gave it to Tom Timothy to read in the first *Boyo* book.
3. Psalm 8:6 KJV - "Thou madest him to have dominion over the works of thy hands; thou hast put all things under his feet."
4. Many shores in northern Maine experience tidal shifts of 10 to 20 feet, depending on the phase of the moon.

CHAPTER 19

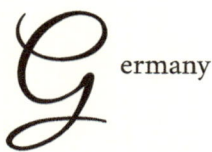ermany

TOM SAT MOTIONLESS, for hours or minutes, he never knew. The small cell might have rocked with an earthquake or flooded with a deluge from the distant heavens, but Tom's oblivion, his stupor of insensibility, was absolute. He only saw the word lit up behind his eyelids, only heard it reverberate continuously in his mind.

Peace

As he huddled in the dirt and darkness, a casualty of an international conflict on a worldwide scale never seen before, a word had been given to him, personally to him. A word that both shamed and reassured him, a word from his youth, a promise he had rejected.

Peace

Surely the infection and injury to his arm, the concussion to his brain, his disorientation in the dark cell, surely this fusion of disparate elements was causing these delusions and hallucinations. There was no blanket or first aid kit, no water or bread, no Bible or word of consolation. He was dying in the wreckage of his plane, or he was already in hell, tantalized by hope and memories as ethereal as dancing dust motes in a streak of sunlight. He fell back onto the dirt.

Peace

Eyes opened or closed made no difference; darkness reigned. The pain in his body assured him that he had not entered his father's heaven. Crushing despair, an immovable weight upon his chest was only alleviated by flitting memories of the good moments in his life. Ruth dancing with him; Tom Timothy in his arms, smelling of innocence; his mother's love for him radiating from her in waves; his father's hand warm and firm on his shoulder. But other images fought for a place in his consciousness. He watched himself receive every rejection and every hurt, every slight and every disappointment, every broken promise and every loss.

Peace

The word would not leave Tom, would not release him from life, would not stop his breath. The word hovered in the atmosphere, echoing and repeating until his mind could take no more.

Isn't waking up a choice? Don't I have enough free will to open my eyes only if I choose, to listen only if I wish? He questioned himself feverishly.

Tom's body tensed. Something was touching his face, something was here, and he had no weapons except for fear and anger. His body tried to tense, to coil, to strike, but weakness sapped his energy, and he lay listless.

Freed. He heard it whispered in a soft guttural voice. *Freed* was whispered again. Tom felt his fever rage, yet the refrain of the word *Freed* offered a coolness, a respite.

His eyes opened involuntarily at the noise, and he watched in horrified wonder as a being ascended out of his cell. Then darkness fell again.

He woke as a dim sunlight filtered down and lightened some of his shadowed surroundings. He was warm, and the fever seemed to have left him. He struggled to a sitting position, leaning against fresh hay piled at the wall behind his back. He quickly looked around the small space. Once again, there was a covered cloth at his feet. And a clean chamber pot and more clean cloths next to a basin of water and a sliver of what might be soap. Tom gently shook his head in wonder. The Bible still lay open. He remembered his most recent vision, a being ascending through the barn floor above him.

He tentatively reached for the Bible, picking it up gently as though it might dissolve in his hands. It was open to the same page, but now there was more charcoal, another word linked to the original circled word.

Frieden

It was the word the being, he wouldn't call it an angel though it did seem merciful in its dealings with him, kept whispering to him. The word was foreign, the voice unfamiliar, but he had sensed no malevolence, no aggression.

Frieden

Tom carefully returned the Bible to its exact spot by the wall as he whispered the word over and over to himself. When the being had spoken to him, it sounded as though the ending "n" sound was swallowed up. He tried to repeat the word as the being had said it: *Friede*

He dipped one of the cloths in the clean water and wiped his face, rubbing briskly, trying to bring back his sharp and logical vision, the analytical mindset he had adopted since he went to college. There had to be a logical explanation, a scientific reason, for all that was happening to him. In his physical and mental weakness, he had fallen back on the stories of his father and the Bible, simplistic attempts to make sense of the universe.

Superstition and empty prayers to an unknown and unknowable deity weren't worth his time or energy. He needed to control himself and his space. He was the only one who could care for his injuries now.

He took a breath and steeled himself to see the wound, possibly gangrenous by now, that covered his left arm, from the edge of his shoulder through his bicep and into the bend of his elbow. A wave of nausea swept over him as he imagined the pain to come. Ironically, now that he felt a bit better, he would need to hurt himself more, to dig out the infection to keep his arm.[1]

He calmed his breath and relaxed his stomach. Though he was hungry, he feared vomiting up the food his body craved and needed desperately. First a little surgery and then breakfast, he promised himself. "You can do it, Tom, you must do it!" he whispered to himself as he shifted his injured arm into one of the thin shafts of sunlight breaking through from above.

He carefully began to lift the neatly folded cloth, wondering again at his spotty memory—when did he take the time or where did he gain the skill to arrange a bandage so expertly. As he removed the cloth, he gasped at the sight—his shoulder was a mass of green, foaming green.

---

1. Experience taught surgeons that the best way to stop such wounds from getting infected was a technique called debridement—the painful process of cutting away the dead tissue and foreign matter that caused infections in the wound. And it's a technique that is still used today.

CHAPTER 20

$\mathcal{M}$aine

August 21, 1943

Grandfather knew how to efficiently run his saltwater farm and how to make a great stew, but he needed me sometimes to remind him about other important things, like justice. We'd enjoyed our supper, talking about the seal and how well he swam, how the minnows I'd caught must have strengthened him, even a little bit about how God had answered Grandfather's prayer. I had so many questions, some I could ask and some I was afraid to. But I figured that after today's adventure, Grandfather would see I'd grown up and needed to know more. It had been a life and death type of day, and in the books I'd read back in Brooklyn, stressful times, especially times with guns (even if they weren't fired), usually led to secrets being revealed.

"Does God always give you what you ask for, Grandfather? Does he always answer your prayer so quickly and clearly like he did today?" I asked, pushing my empty dish to the side.

He swept a pile of crumbs onto his empty plate and set it aside, then looked at me. "God always hears his people's prayers, Tom Timothy, always. But don't think of God like Santa Claus to bring you gifts or some genie to grant your wishes," he answered.

82

"Well, what about this afternoon? Didn't your God hear and answer your request?" I persisted.

"He did indeed. Seeing that seal swim off was a beautiful sight I'll never forget, and I'm so grateful that God acted today. But I bring many prayers, requests, and concerns to God every day, and many of them I bring over and over. I know He hears me, listens to my pleas, but sometimes He chooses not to give me what I ask for."

I nodded—I could understand asking for lots of things. "But I'll bet he gives you the important stuff always, right?" I figured I was beginning to understand Grandfather and his God.

"No, Tom Timothy, not always. Honestly, if He had answered my most important prayers as I wished, your grandmother would still be with me, and I'd never have lost your father." His voice broke slightly, and he stared down at his hands.

Jumping up, shock swept over me first, which was quickly followed by anger. "Your God did not hear your prayers about Grandmother? He let my grandmother die? And still you believe in him and follow him? I don't understand, Grandfather, not at all!" I shook my head back and forth. "And not only that, but he let you lose your only son! What kind of God is that?"

Grandfather looked so sad for a moment that I was sick with guilt. Why did I have to argue with him about religion? Why did I keep stirring up the hostilities? I saw it then: God was the problem between Father and Grandfather. God was the enemy here.

But was he? God had saved the seal for us; I couldn't deny that fact.

"Sit down, Boyo, please sit down. I understand your anger, I do."

I looked at him, not sure I did. "But weren't you ever angry, too?"

"Of course, angry and heartbroken, devastated really. I was sad for a long time, sad and confused. I know God heals people; He performs miracles; He reaches into human lives and helps. I know that, Boyo, as sure I know you are my grandson sitting at my table."

"But why didn't he help you? I've never had a grandmother, you know. And I almost never had you."

"For a time, Tom Timothy, I raged against God, against His injustice in taking my wife to heaven and letting my son disown me. It wasn't fair because I had tried to follow Him faithfully, to keep my family serving him. I cried out to Him in my anger and frustration. I even questioned His righteousness and justice, His mercy and love."

"You're right, Grandfather, it wasn't fair!"

"No, Tom Timothy, I was wrong. God reminded me of words spoken in one of the oldest accounts in the Bible, by a great but imperfect man. After the worst personal losses imaginable, Job said, 'the LORD gave, and the LORD hath taken away; blessed be the name of the LORD.'"[1] Grandfather rubbed his hands over his face, tugging lightly on his beard. "I realized then, Tom Timothy, that I only questioned the goodness and righteousness of God when He took something away from me. I never wondered if He was right to give me anything in the first place. Do you understand?"

I shook my head, no; I wasn't sure I even wanted to understand. Goodness and righteousness, giving and taking—no, I didn't understand.

Grandfather whispered some strange words, then leaned forward and looked into my eyes. "Your grandmother Liz was such a gift to me—she was smarter, kinder, prettier, godlier than I ever deserved. God gave us over twenty-five years together, and much of that time I wasted. And your father? Why, Tom was such a wonderful boy, so smart, strong, honorable, good. I never deserved a son like that! I tried to be a worthy father to him, I tried to honor my wife, I tried, and I failed often. But I never questioned God's goodness or justice for giving a broken man like me such a wife and son, for giving me a saltwater farm that fed my body and spirit, for giving me this life. No, in my pride and ignorance, I felt I deserved them. I forgot that every good and perfect thing in my life is from God: Liz, Tom, Bethel, and you! Boyo, I don't deserve to be your grandfather—God is so extravagant in His love and mercy to have let me know you for this summer! He gives, and sometimes He takes away. Blessed is the name of the Lord!" He sat back and breathed deeply.

The kitchen was silent except for the sounds of the cooling stove. I had so much to think about. I got up from my side of the table and crossed over to stand beside Grandfather. I had nothing to say, but I think he was okay that I just leaned against him.

84

1. Job 1:21 – And said, Naked came I out of my mother's womb, and naked shall I return thither: the Lord gave, and the Lord hath taken away; blessed be the name of the Lord (KJV).

CHAPTER 21

$\mathcal{M}$aine

We were both quiet the next morning, silent at breakfast except for Grandfather's words of thanks. I was washing up when he finally broke the silence. "Do you want to ride into town with me and Balaam? I need to pick up the truck, the mail, and some groceries. I'm also going to find Leo Gagnon and talk to him about the seal. It won't be pleasant going to his place, so I understand if you'd rather stay home."

"I'd like to come, Grandfather. I can even drive Balaam if you'd like to sit back and enjoy the scenery. You can be a man of leisure for a bit instead of a saltwater farmer."

He chuckled, "'A man of leisure'—ha! Finish your chores, and we'll head in; it looks like a storm later tonight."

The dishes were done in minutes, and the barn was acceptable after an hour of shoveling and sweeping. I'd mucked a bit slower to keep myself cleaner because I didn't have time to do much washing up, and the stream was too cold when the winds blew and the clouds blocked the sun. I scrubbed my hands, sniffed deeply, and passed my personal manure test.

I quickly wrote Mother a note; I knew she'd want to tell Gio about the

86

seal miracle. I'd had so many adventures in Maine that Gio would be entertained for a year. Mother too, but she wouldn't appreciate the scars. Hopefully a letter from Mother would come with news of Father.

Grandfather had harnessed Balaam to the wagon, and he handed me the reins as I climbed up to the seat. I clicked my teeth and gave the reins a little flick, just like Grandfather, and Balaam started down the drive.

"Have you any letters to mail today, Tom Timothy?"

"Yes, Grandfather, I have a short note for Mother. I had to tell her about the seal and its marvelous healing. She'll find it fascinating, and Gio will find it exciting. I know you can't tell me about Mother's letters to you, but I'm a bit worried about her. Her letters are getting shorter, and she just seems sad. It's a good thing I'm going back soon, Grandfather; I think she misses me too much."

"I'm sure she does, Boyo, and I know I will miss you when you go. Who'll make sure I can ride to town as a man of leisure?"

As we turned toward town, I only had one question for Grandfather: what about the moose? The morning after the attack, he'd taught me how to dodge a moose on foot (put a big rock or tree between you and the moose), but what would I do while driving Balaam? I asked him as I glanced nervously into the woods that blanketed each side of the road.

"Dawn and dusk are the dangerous times, Tom Timothy. Keep a lookout and know that Balaam is very aware of smells as well. We'll have no problem today; I'm sure of it." I decided to borrow some of his confidence and started to whistle.

About a mile outside of town, Grandfather told me to pull down a narrow drive, overgrown with weeds and overhung by firs and broken-branched maples. The clear sea-washed air seemed to disappear, and I was reminded of the dark and oppressive alleys of New York.

"This is the Gagnon place, but never come here without me[1]. They're not too friendly, and they'd just as soon fight you as wish you good morning." As soon as a ramshackle building became visible, three dogs of various shapes and sizes rushed the wagon, growling and snapping at Balaam's hooves. Grandfather jumped down, shouting "Hey, git on" at the dogs and waving his coat. "Keep going, Boyo, keep going," Grandfather told me as the dogs slunk off. I stopped in front of the dilapidated house.

A man with a shotgun cocked over his arm walked off the porch toward

87

Grandfather. His clothes were filthy, and greasy, gray hair straggled over his shoulders. His eyes were mean and bloodshot.

"What brings you to my land, Joshua?" he spat at Grandfather's feet.

"Good morning, Leo. This is my grandson, Tom Timothy."

The man spat again after giving me a disgusted glance.

"What, Joshua?"

"A seal was shot, Len, and it crept up on my shore. It's hide was badly torn by a shot gun."

"What do I care? A seal means nothing to me."

"I thought you might have a word with your boys. It's not good to wound animals and then leave them to die. You know a wounded creature can be vicious."

"Why're you blaming my boys? You got some nerve coming here," he growled.

"I'm not accusing them, Leo, just mentioning it. They might have thought the seal was bothering their traps or something. I'm just hoping you'd speak to them."

"Traps!" He spat again. "They're too stinkin' lazy to set a trap, but ..." he paused, giving Grandfather a sly look, "at least they haven't deserted me and the family homestead. At least they're loyal."

At that moment, I jumped in my seat and covered my stinging cheek. An acorn lay in my lap, and I looked over and saw two boys about my age, smirking and waving a slingshot at me as they hid in the over-grown hedge. I slowly looked away from them, not letting them see any reaction, just like Gio taught me. My cheek burned, but I decided not to tell Grandfather—I'd be gone soon, and those boys would never bother me again.

"Thanks for your time, Leo. I appreciate your talking to your boys." He turned to me and quietly said, "Let's go, Tom Timothy, now."

"Git, Joshua, or I'll sic the dogs on you!" he shouted at our backs.

When we were finally rid of the Gagnon place and back on the main road, I assured Grandfather. "I'll never go there—I've never seen so much spit in my life. Disgusting!" He laughed and patted my shoulder. Then with a serious look, he said, "Something or someone wounded that man, and now he's as vicious and dangerous as any hurt creature. Stay clear of him."

The rest of the trip was pleasant: the truck was ready, and we each got mail. Grandfather sent me out to the wagon with the groceries, but he came out of the store within five minutes. I wasn't sure why, but he looked very serious. Probably it was just the Gagnon effect.

Balaam made good time, and I did a great job driving. Grandfather followed behind me in the truck. He stopped me as I was about to turn into Bethel. "Let's make a quick visit to Miss Rachel; I want to make sure she's ready for the storm." He left the truck inside the gate. It wasn't dusk yet, so I happily kept driving.

When we got to Miss Rachel's, Grandfather called out a greeting. We heard her out in back, probably puttering in her garden. Her vegetables were close to finished, but she still had plenty of herbs and flowers.

"Afternoon, boys," Miss Rachel welcomed us as we came around the house.

"It's fixing to storm tonight, don't you think, Rachel?" Grandfather asked, his thick eyebrows questioned her, but he didn't smile. Then he turned to me, "Tom Timothy, please take Balaam and pump some fresh water for him in the trough. Now."

I headed off to take care of the horse; I wanted Balaam rested and watered in case we encountered any critters on the way home. I looked back and saw Grandfather had his hand on Miss Rachel's shoulder and was talking intensely but quietly. He handed her a crumpled letter from his pocket. She read it silently, looked up at him, and handed it back. She then glanced back and gave me a little wave. She looked worried rather than happy. Quite a storm must be coming

---

1. Derived from old French *gagnon* "guard dog". The name most likely originated as a nickname for an aggressive or cruel person (https://surnames.behindthename.com/name/gagnon).

CHAPTER 22

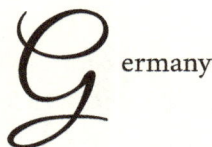ermany

HE STARTED to gag as memories of the wretched smell of gangrene rose to his consciousness. Despite the nursing staff's best efforts, a nauseating haze of decaying flesh hung over the hospital ward where he'd visited his injured friends. He'd tried to keep his face neutral, but the sight of so many missing arms and legs horrified him. Now this— his own arm rotting! "Dear God!" slipped out of his mouth before he could stop it.

But his empty stomach slowed his retching, and he was startled by another odor in his cell, possibly even rising from his shoulder. Warily, he turned his head toward his wound and sniffed. Pine! Pine like the woods surrounding his childhood farm! Pine—another sign that he was slipping into madness.

Pine? He was in a closed cell and somehow his wound was slathered in crushed pine needles and sticky pine sap. He gently prodded his shoulder, relieved that the pain was less. Pine? He remembered now; his godmother, Rachel, had told him that clean

90

pine sap and resin were some of God's antibiotics, kept right in the woods, part of the heavenly medicine chest. And salt water—Mother was a big believer in the healing powers of salt water. It was funny but he never resented when Rachel or Mother talked about God about His hidden gifts and treasures. They had loved him and God they had embodied the unconditional love people long to receive. But Father, he was the justice of God, the harsh and demanding God who couldn't abide the sin of men. He knew it was immature to make such generalizations about the abstract qualities of God—he was an engineer, a pilot, not a child!

But God's medicine chest had failed his mother, taken her before her only son could even kiss her goodbye or thank her. God and his father had failed him there, failed him and his mother!

His mind was so jumbled—why waste time thinking about his father now? The old farmer certainly never thought of him. Why, he was a pagan, the prodigal son in the flesh. But rebellion and revenge didn't feel so rewarding laying on a dirt floor losing one's mind. Tom snorted sarcastically.

What about the pine? He'd just left it on his arm—it smelled better than rotting flesh. He reached for the water; he was always so thirsty. Why was he so thirsty? He wasn't sweating or feverish any longer. Why did he always fall asleep after eating and drinking?

His heart began to race, and now he was sweating. Was he being drugged? Was paranoia part and parcel of the madness that seemed to be taking over his mind. He put the water down and laid back. Would he rather live as a madman or die with sanity? Were those his only choices? What about Ruth and Tom Timothy? He wanted to yell with frustration, shout out his anger and fear. But he remembered the boots and smashing guns, the urgent whispers. He needed to stay silent, yes, but he didn't need to drink all the water, just a sip or two. He carefully poured the rest into the chamber pot.

Tom laid back down, covering himself with the blankets. He didn't want to sleep, and the cold dirt floor was helpfully uncomfortable. He wanted to remember. He also wanted answers, answers that would prove his sanity or plunge him into permanent madness. Anything was better than this limbo.

He began chanting in his mind: Thomas Freeman, P-51 Mustang pilot, loyal member of the United States Air Force, husband of Ruth, father of Tom Timothy, son of Lizzie and, and of Joshua. He repeated it four times.

Now here's my story: I left the British base with my squadron to escort a recon plane over a classified part of Germany.[1] *The Messerschmitts attacked after we'd finished the recon mission and turned back toward England; they outnumbered us. After I saw one of our planes was hit down, I decided to peel off and act as a decoy. It worked, and three planes followed me. I shot down two of them as I sped toward the northeast. The other Messerschmitt flew off into Germany, not noticing that my plane took a fatal hit—the coolant line. I knew I only had minutes to get low before the engine seized. I could see fields below, farmland like my father's. I tried to glide.*

I was only just above the treetops when the plane dropped. I tried to land, but I must admit I crashed. I must have blacked out upon impact, but my next memory was so vivid due to the pain. I was being dragged out of the cockpit, my left arm wedged between the seat and the broken window. I felt my arm rip apart. Dumped on the ground next to my plane, I saw a figure running about. The heat was rising, and I knew the plane would explode any moment, my faithful flying gas tank! As I tried to crawl away, my collar was grabbed and I was dragged to a cooler spot, but then the nightmare began. I was stripped of my shirt, pants, and jacket, and then I saw the dirty face, soot-steaked and ravaged. The pain in my arm was so great and my mind so disoriented that I couldn't fight back. Then I saw him again, half dragging a body over the ground. He put my clothes on the figure and then threw him into the burning plane. I started to shout, but the fury on his face silenced me. Then he came back and grabbed my dog tags and my blood chit. I tried to fight back then, but his blow must have knocked me out. The sucker punch came from the same person, the face I'll never forget. That's my story. I must remember it, not the insanity that is surrounding me now. That is the reality I know.

A sound disturbed Tom, bringing him back to the reality of his cell. *I must remain still, not give anything away.* Tom forced his breathing to stay slow and steady. Someone was here, walking around him. He heard the dripping sound of water poured into the clay pot and felt the blankets adjusted over his feet. There was so little noise that he

92

wondered if he was hallucinating, but then he felt a breath, human breath, as someone lifted the bandage to check his arm. Tom's eyes opened, and in the semi-darkness saw! It was him! The killer! They stared in each other's eyes, equally startled. Tom inhaled, about to scream, but the killer covered Tom's nose and mouth with his hand and shook his head. Tom was too weak to throw him off, but he wouldn't give up. Who was this suffocating fiend? Tom didn't give up, not until the darkness overtook him.

---

1. "The North American P-51 Mustang is the gold standard for WWII fighters...A long-range escort fighter was needed not only to bring the bombers in and out of Germany, but also to wrestle control of the sky from the German fighters who preyed on the bombers. The Mustang, with its high speed, long-range, low-cost, and six .50 caliber M2 Browning machine guns, made it the ideal fighter for the job" (https://www.nationalww2museum.org/war/articles/north-american-p-51-mustang).

CHAPTER 23

$\mathcal{N}$ ew York City

EACH DAY WAS A BLUR, dim at best, with nothing to make it any more memorable than the previous dark day. Only Tom Timothy's letters were the exception—reading about her boy's adventures brightened the room, and some of her child's vitality seemed to seep into her fingertips as she handled his carefully penned notes.

But she knew it wasn't enough, not powerful enough to keep the darkness at bay. And she feared she'd drain the joy and energy from her boy, and that would be an unforgivable sin.

Dearest Tom,

I've made my decision; I cannot be a good mother to our Tom Timothy—I know it. I've tried to be strong, but I only grow weaker each day.

I've decided to put my final efforts into prayer for

you and your return. Yes, prayer, Tom! There's nothing else I can do to bring you home. There are no logical actions, no scientific methods, only petitions on my knees to the God we have both neglected for so long. I am empty of everything else, just a love for you and Tom Timothy and our little girl. I think of her all the time. So, as you see, prayer is my only resource, my only hope.

I pray you still have my Bible. I know now that it was the greatest gift I could ever give you other than my love and our children.

I'm begging God for your safety, Tom, for your heart and its strength. Please remember the truths you grew up with.

Your Ruth

ADDING the letter to the stack, she only wept for a moment. She felt, at least for the minutes before she drifted into a deep and exhausted sleep, that she had shared her burden with someone else.

The next evening, her feet ached as she completed the last mile of her walk home from the factory in the deepening dusk. She was late for the boarding house dinner, again. Hopefully, Bridget had saved her a plate, hidden in the kitchen cupboard from Mrs. Shaw's prying eyes. Even cold meat and potatoes would taste good tonight, at least for a bite or two.

Unease swept over her when she saw her landlady on the sidewalk in front of the porch, clearly looking down the street for her. Flushed but weary, Ruth hurried to Mrs. Shaw, dreading her words.

"There's a man in the parlor. He's looking for you. He'd say

95

nothing except that he was looking for you." Her lips were pursed with disapproval.

"For me? I don't know, Mrs. Shaw. I'm sorry. I'll see to it straight away." She looked up into the parlor windows and saw a silhouette, tall and broad-shouldered. She'd know his shadow anywhere! Her breath quickened as memories flooded her mind. Brushing past her landlady, she rushed up the front steps. Ruth fumbled with the front doorknob, then hurried into the parlor, calling "Tom" in a strangled cry.

He turned and stepped into the light. Tom's eyes flashed toward her, but the gray beard and hair betrayed her. "Ruth," spoken in a deep but unknown voice confirmed it.

"You're not Tom" was the broken phrase that spilled with her tears as she collapsed to the floor.

Ruth didn't hear his gruff shout, "Woman, help me here!" nor did she feel him lift her off the floor.

Mrs. Shaw stood in the doorway, shock rendering her speechless for a moment. "What have you done, sir?" she finally blustered, remembering that this was her boardinghouse and Ruth was under her care.

"Clear the sofa of those fancy pillows and bring me some smelling salts and a damp cloth," the man thundered, but he added a belated "please" as she called Bridget's name.

Scooping her off the floor, Grandfather thought she felt like a child, frail and bird-like. Could this girl be the woman he was searching for? Laying her on the couch, he studied her face, gaunt but beautiful, at peace now but lined with worry and fatigue. His gnarled hand, rough and weather-beaten against her pale, smooth forehead, moved aside the rich brown tresses, and he knew. She was Ruth. Those were Tom Timothy's curls.

He held his breath and fought back his emotions. She was his Boyo's mother and his son's wife. She was his family.

The maid softly jostled his arm, and he stepped aside to let her wave the smelling salts under the girl's nose.

Choking slightly on the pungent fumes, Ruth's eyelids fluttered. Within an instant, her hazel eyes desperately searched the room, quickly finding him as he leaned forward. Her deep look of disappointment hurt him. "You're not Tom," she whispered again. "But your silhouette? Your eyes?" There was wonder and confusion in her voice.

He gently touched her arm. "No, I'm not. I'm sorry, but I'm not. I'm Joshua, Thomas's father."

She started up, fear flooding all her features. "Oh no, Tom Timothy!" she cried out.

"He's fine, Tom Timothy is fine, safe in Maine. He is with our friend, Miss Rachel. Remember, Tom Timothy wrote you about her." He tried to keep his voice calm.

As she sat back, she became even paler, but her hysteria seemed to be replaced by an even more dangerous lethargy.

"Call a doctor, Miss. Call a doctor now," instructed Joshua.

He was surprised to hear a response from the body on the sofa. "No, no doctors. Promise me no doctors," she weakly implored.

Joshua nodded his agreement, but then he knelt beside her. "I promise no doctors if you'll drink some broth and eat some food. Now, not later, now." His voice was gentle but firm.

When Ruth quietly agreed and closed her eyes, Bridget hurried to the kitchen to warm some broth and heat up the hidden plate.

Mrs. Shaw cleared her throat, and Joshua moved aside as the landlady gently covered the young woman with a warm shawl.

Once they both observed Ruth sleeping, Joshua pointed to the hallway where the proprietress joined him.

"Thank you for your help. What ails the girl?"

"Ruth works long hours at the munitions factory and worries constantly about her flier husband and her boy that she sent away. I've tried to get her to eat more, but she misses too many meals. I've never seen her this weak before." Joshua could hear the worry and sincerity in her voice.

"I understand. These are hard times, especially for wives and mothers." He cleared his throat. "Is her rent paid? Does she have any debts that you know of?"

"No, Ruth's a responsible girl in every way. Except for missing meals, she's one of my best boarders." She looked at him closely. "Why do you ask?"

"I'm Ruth's father-in-law. I've come to take her home, to Maine and to her son. Please have your girl pack up her belongings. We'll be leaving as soon as we can." He nodded his head and returned to watch over the sleeping form.

True to her word, Ruth drank the broth and ate the warmed-up dinner when she awakened. She leaned on Joshua's arm as they slowly and silently mounted the stairs to her room.

"I'm sending up Bridget to make sure you're comfortable. I will see you tomorrow," Joshua said as he turned to leave.

"Thank you," she whispered.

He lifted his hand toward her: "Be strong, Ruth, and of good courage."[1] Then she heard his boots descend the stairs.

---

1. An allusion to Joshua 1:7 "Only be thou strong and very courageous" (KJV).

CHAPTER 24

New York City

Awakening in the late morning with a throbbing headache, Ruth lay disoriented, unable to drive the images from her mind. She'd dreamt of Tom again, that he'd come home to her. She'd seen his back; she knew those shoulders, and with his head cocked back and his hands jammed in his pockets, she was positive it was her Tom. The dream was so real, but the disappointment was even sharper—her chest still ached from it.

The clock chimed from Mrs. Shaw's sitting room: 9 bells! She was late, so late. She'd be fired for sure, and she didn't even care. She was too tired to rise from the bed, too tired to dress and descend to the dining room. Perhaps this was a sign that she was finished at the factory, finished with everything.

The knock at the door startled her; it was too tentative for Mrs. Shaw, and Bridget always loudly announced herself. "Yes?" her voice was weak. "I'm so tired. Please go away."

The knock was a little louder, and a man spoke! A man? Mrs. Shaw would never let a man up the stairs to her room.

"Excuse me, may I come in?" he said again, the door barely cracked.

She pulled the quilt to her chin; curiosity had driven away some of the crushing fatigue. "Yes, you may," she replied, watching the door closely.

A big work-hardened hand pushed the door open, and a worn boot entered. When a tall man, gray on his head and beard followed, she gasped. He looked like the man from her hazy dream. He quickly glanced up, and she cried out when she saw his bright blue eyes.

"You're him, from my dream!" Her voice was quiet but choked by emotion.

"It wasn't a dream. I was here yesterday, Ruth. May I call you Ruth?" he asked. When she nodded, he pulled up the only chair in the room, sat down, and clasped his hands.

"I'm Joshua, Thomas's father."

She stared in disbelief, but then she sat up in a panic, her eyes darting about frantically. "Tom Timothy, my boy, where is he? Where is my son?"

He hastened to answer, trying to calm her. "The boy is fine, safe in Maine. He is with my friend, his friend too, Miss Rachel. I promise, he is well and strong and happy, but he misses you greatly."

Her hazel eyes, filled with unshed tears, had turned a bright green. They searched his face desperately.

He handed her a mug of water which she only used to wet her lips. "If Tom Timothy is fine, then why are you here, Joshua?" her voice trembled. "Why?"

"I came because of your letters. They troubled me."

"I didn't ask you to come. I didn't. I asked you to take Tom Timothy, to be his guardian, to raise him. I told you there was money, money for his care, money for his education. I didn't ask you to come." She buried her face in her hands, and he could barely hear her question as she wept. "Don't you want him?"

Joshua's hands quickly but gently clasped her hands, pulling them down. "That's not it, Ruth."

She shut her eyes tightly and shook her head, pleading not only with the old man but with the universe. "Is it because of his lip? It's

100

not important, it won't stop him in life. Please, he's smart, he's ..." her sobs stopped her.

"Ruth, Ruth, look at me, Ruth," Joshua's deep voice was hard to ignore. He put a clean but well-worn handkerchief into her hands, and she gripped it tightly.

After a moment, she looked up, and Joshua's heart nearly broke. He'd never seen a sadder woman, not even his Liz when she was so sick.

"Hear me, Ruth. Listen to me." His voice was gruff with emotion. "I love Tom Timothy. He's a wonderful boy, smart and full of life, so much like Thomas that it sometimes startles me. He's a gift to me, girl, a true blessing." His voice softened, "But you can't give him to me. I think he's grown fond of me these months, maybe even loves his grandfather, but he doesn't want me. He wants you, you and Thomas."

"You truly care for him, Joshua, truly? For the boy he is, not just for the man you want him to become?" she asked, her eyes probing him for the truth.

Joshua winced, hearing his sins with Thomas so clearly spoken. But he refused to make excuses now; she was right to worry. He looked at her earnestly. "Yes, truly. Why, he's turned my orderly world upside down, asked me questions that would baffle the greatest theologians, challenged me, shown me a world I'd forgotten to see and sounds I no longer heard. And he makes me laugh. I can't imagine my world without that boy, my Boyo." He blinked back tears of his own.

Her eyes sparkled with joy for an instant as she pictured her son's relationship with his grandfather. But then a cloud seemed to pass over her. "If you're happy with him, Joshua, why did you come? I told you I cannot be his mother any longer. Look at me."

"You look too thin and too tired, but food and rest will strengthen you," Joshua argued.

"No, I'm too weak. Too weak in spirit and mind to be a good mother to Tom Timothy. When the darkness comes over me, I can barely breathe. I can't think or hardly care for myself, much less a child. My thoughts are unhealthy and frightening. I could never expose my boy to this"—she waved her hand over herself—"never." Her hand dropped listlessly to the bed.

101

"Why such despair, Ruth, such certainty that this is your future?"

"I've been in this state once before, this prison of depression and darkness. Doctors took our money and gave me drugs, but I nearly died, nearly lost my mind. Only Tom was able to save me. But he's not here now."

"When did this happen, Ruth? Was there a reason?" His eyes, as tender as Tom's, eased her reticence.

"Fourteen years ago come December, I was sick for nearly a year. Our baby died, you see. We never talked about it, and we chose to never tell Tom Timothy. He didn't need to know that death had taken his sister before she even had a chance to breathe on this earth."

"A little girl?" breathed Joshua softly.

"Yes, Lizzie. Little Lizzie, I miss her so."

Upon hearing her name, tears spilled from Joshua's eyes as well, and he gathered Ruth into his arms as though she were just a child, a heart-broken child. He rocked her as he had rocked Thomas so many years ago.

When their tears were finished, he laid her back on the pillows. She took a strange comfort in his grief-ravaged face.

"I'm so sorry, Ruth, I never knew." Pain and regret twisted his features.

"Oh, Joshua, do you think she is with God?"

"Yes, my dear, I know she is. She is with God and her grandmother. I know because He is a loving and merciful God."

Ruth reached for his hand and held it. "But the darkness is coming back, closer and more powerful than before. Please take Timothy; I can't recover this time. I can't recover, I can't, certainly not without Tom." Her voice and demeanor were resigned. Her eyes were empty of hope.

"But Thomas is just missing, he could . . ." Joshua began.

Ruth quietly interrupted him. "Three weeks ago, they sent a letter. His plane went down, and they have his tags. There is no body to bury, just his dog tags."

Joshua had paled at the news, but he bowed his head and whispered words that Ruth could not understand. Then he stood. "Ruth, we cannot know everything. We cannot believe everything that this world tells us. My friend, Miss Rachel, is a healer and sometimes prophetic[1]. She speaks with the Lord and hears His words. She told me before I left to come to you that Thomas is alive. He is hurt and struggling, but he is alive."

"But Tom doesn't beli..." began Ruth.

"Thomas may have given up God, but God has not given up Thomas. We must keep praying, Ruth, praying fiercely. And you must not give up either. Right now, your son has lost his father, at least for a time, but he cannot lose his mother. The war appears to have taken Thomas from the boy, and that is a heavy load he bears. But if his mother abandons him, I believe it will crush him."

---

1. Here is evidence of Miss Rachel's and Grandfather's belief in the gift of prophecy as found in 1 Corinthians 14:3– "On the other hand, the one who prophesies speaks to people for their upbuilding and encouragement and consolation" (ESV).

CHAPTER 25

*N*ew York City

"EXCUSE ME, sir. I've brought up some tea and toast," said Bridget in a hushed tone. She blushed at Joshua's smile of thanks.

"I'll come back later, Ruth. Eat and rest," said Joshua on his way out of the room.

At the bottom of the stairs, he found a restless Mrs. Shaw. "I sent Bridget with a light breakfast. She'll help Ruth get washed up." The woman paced to the front door and back, then she turned to Joshua. "What are your plans, sir? I'm fond of the girl, but I haven't the facilities or time to get her well and then nurse her back to strength." Her mouth was set in a firm line, but she wouldn't look in Joshua's eyes.

"I understand, Mrs. Shaw, I do. It is time for family to help her, to care for her. As I said yesterday, I'm taking her home to Maine, to the family farm. Her boy is there—it will be a wonderful reunion, I'm sure."

Her shoulders relaxed; she'd expected judgment, not understanding. "Bridget can help her pack up. And she can take her meals in her room—those stairs can be tiring."

Joshua nodded. "Thank you, Mrs. Shaw. That is very kind. Now, I've a favor or two to ask of you, if you have a moment."

Twenty minutes later, Joshua was out in the streets of Brooklyn. The directions were clear, and he quickly found the tenement, an old building set back only a few feet from the dirty street. He shook his head. How did people live without fields and forests? Without woods and water? The buildings and brick pressed upon him from all sides, and to rid himself of an encroaching claustrophobia, he forced himself to breathe deeply. He coughed—the air itself was tainted by exhaust, smoke, and sewage. How did they breathe without the cleansing drafts of pine and salt water? How could Thomas live here? Joshua shook his head sadly and walked toward the worn, cement stoop.

The front door opened into a small, dark vestibule which led to a hallway on the left and steep stairs on the right. He checked the scribbled notes clutched in his left hand. Fourth floor. He started climbing. If only all the miles he'd ploughed behind Balaam had prepared him for this emotional trudge. With each step up, the impressions got stronger. Human bodies, too many human bodies, in a cramped space—he shuddered at the memory of the transport ship to France, he and all the other doughboys crammed together, barely enough room to breathe for a boy from the open spaces of Maine. And then from the ship to the war front. He shuddered at the remembrance of the filthy cold and endless mud of the trenches, still sickened by the thought of the times his bullets and bayonet had found their targets. He had tried to keep those memories away, far away from thoughts of his son. He stopped to lean his forehead against the wall. "Dear God, protect him, my son, my Thomas!" Joshua kept climbing.

The stairs ended at the fourth floor—no carpet or rug covered the scratched and worn landing, but it was clean. It smelled better here; he inhaled a richness of spices, onions and garlic and tomatoes, he thought. Taking a deep breath, he knocked firmly on the door.

It took a moment, but the door finally swung open. Joshua saw no one until a little face, at the level of his knee, peeked out. Joshua tried to look friendly, but he felt a deep tension—he had to get this right

105

"Mamma! Mamma!" cried the child, a boy with big brown eyes and masses of curls. "Mamma!"

Clearly the child saw only the tension. Joshua cleared his throat and waited as a small woman dressed in black approached him. He saw the worry on her face. She waited expectantly.

"Gio," said Joshua. "I want to see Gio." The worry turned to fear on the woman's face as she grasped the door with one hand and moved the little boy behind her with the other.

"No," she shook her head. "No, Gio *malato*, sick." Her small body blocked the doorway, and the fierceness in her eyes reminded Joshua of the protective maternal instinct throughout nature. She might have been a fierce mother badger guarding her den, protecting her young.

Joshua lifted his hands and hurried to explain. "Ruth?"

The woman's eyes narrowed, but she did not shift her defensive position.

"Tom Timothy?" Then, he patted his chest and said, "Grandfather."

She looked closely into his eyes and began to relax. "*Nonno?* Tom Timothy, *Nonno?*" Her face broke into a beautiful smile of welcome. "*Buongiorno!*" she said, opening the door widely and waving him in. She pointed to a small sofa that nearly filled the room and said, "*Solo un minuto*" as she hurried toward a curtained area. He could hear an excited exchange, a cadence of Italian words flowing behind the curtain. The little boy stood still by the door, just staring.

He turned away from the child as he heard the curtain drawn back. The woman waved him forward and pointed toward the bed: "Gio, Gio."

Dark eyes peered out under unruly black curls, suspicious eyes that questioned Joshua. "Who are you?" said the boy, a strong voice projecting from his thin body.

"I'm Joshua, Tom Timothy's grandfather. And you are Gio, yes?" Joshua extended his right hand to the boy and smiled.

Gio slowly reached out and shook hands; the boy struggled to put strength into his grip. Joshua saw the silent exertion pass over the boy's face and liked him the better for it.

"I've heard about you, from Tom Timothy's letters." The boy was still wary. "Are you looking out for him, are you?" Gio's concern for his friend was clear.

"Well, I'd say we are watching out for each other," replied Joshua.

That was good enough for Gio, and the boy grinned. "Good," he said with a nod.

"Where is Tom Timothy?" asked Gio. "Have you brought him back? School is starting soon"—he pointed toward his body—"I'll probably be ready to start with him. We always walk together, over and back; it's safer that way."

"Tom Timothy's still in Maine; he'll be staying longer." Joshua saw the light fade in Gio's eyes. "But he misses you, talks about you all the time. Why, once you're up to it, you'll need to come up and see him."

Gio smiled slightly, but his disappointment couldn't be hidden. His face grew suddenly serious—he looked like a man now, not a boy. "But what about his mamma? She is not well, I know. She says she's okay when she visits me, but I know, my mamma knows."

"You are both right, Gio, she is not well. I am taking her back to Maine, back to Tom Timothy. We can care for her there. She can rest there."

The tension left Gio's face, and he said, "That is good." He called his mother, rattled off rapid words in Italian, and the woman nodded her head, "Si, si, Gio. Buono!" She gave Joshua a look of approval.

"Gio," continued Joshua, "I need your help."

The boy nodded, his dark eyes unwavering.

"When Tom Timothy's father comes back from the war, please tell him that his family is in Maine, at the farm. Please?" asked Joshua.

"Yes, I will tell him," Gio assured him. "I will make sure my mamma and papa know. I will even tell some of the other neighbors. Tom Timothy's father will know where his family is, I promise."

"Thank you, Gio. Thank you for being such a good friend to Tom Timothy. But," he smiled at the boy, "forget about the fruit next time, okay?"

Gio winced for a moment, remembering the gang that had attacked him for stealing a few apples from their territory, then smiled, nodding with his black eyes twinkling.

Joshua placed one hand on Gio's head and lifted his other hand

107

and voice in thanksgiving, asking for the boy's healing, the knitting of bones and tissues.[1] Gio's mother sighed softly and crossed herself. Joshua then smiled at the family and left.

---

1. Grandfather shows belief in the gift of healing as he blesses Gio. James 5:16 "Therefore confess your sins to each other and pray for each other so that you may be healed. The prayer of a righteous person is powerful and effective" (NIV).

CHAPTER 26

$\mathcal{M}$aine

August 31, 1943

Morning ablutions at the pump with Miss Rachel's sweet lavender soap—I was getting used to a new routine. This was my fourth day at her house, and I was still amazed that her privy smelled so good. I'd have to talk Grandfather into planting some lavender and lilacs around his outhouse!

Speaking of Grandfather, when was he coming back? Don't get me wrong, staying with Miss Rachel was grand: I was more comfortable, had extra time to write in my journal, and loved the food. But where was Grandfather? The harvest time was coming, coming soon. Grandfather had been talking about it for days, and now he was gone! It made no sense.

Miss Rachel and I drove to Bethel each morning and evening to milk the cows and collect the eggs, but even a city boy could tell that summer was packing her bag and getting ready to leave Maine for the winter.

Today, the sky looked gray, and I felt worry swell up inside me: first Father went missing, then Mother sent me away and her letters faded, like she wasn't really there anymore, and now Grandfather! A coldness gripped my insides that the rays of that weak autumn sun could never reach.

I had spent the first three days helping Miss Rachel prepare her extensive *gardens for winter. I brought hay to cover the perennial herbs and winter vegetables and hauled away the dead and dying summer plants to the compost heap. The first frost hadn't come yet, but it was threatening—I felt a sharper chill each morning. Yesterday, I picked a couple bushels of early apples, then washed the car. Grandfather had his trustworthy old truck, and Miss Rachel had a well-used and well-cared for black jalopy that got her to town and church. Finally, I cleaned and swept out the gardening shed. Later in the day, I was supposed to help her with the guest room, the small space I was sleeping in until Grandfather returned.*

But don't forget the bees!

Miss Rachel, so sweet and kind, kept bees, hundreds of them. About a quarter mile back of the house, there were half a dozen hives to house her "little friends." They were small, but I questioned their friendliness and had nearly a dozen welts to prove it.

As she put a soothing cream on the swollen spots, Miss Rachel had apologized: "I'm so sorry, Tom Timothy, but they are just protecting their homes; they're very territorial, and they didn't recognize your scent."

But the honey was worth it! Since I'd come to stay with Miss Rachel, I'd eaten honey with every meal, and I planned on continuing to do so. It was the least those little bugs could do for me.

With my hands clean and smelling good, I splashed my face with the icy pump water. I couldn't help sputtering and shivering; even though I knew it would be cold, it always startled me. I quickly dried off with the clean towel she set out for me every morning. It was breakfast time.

Hurrying into the kitchen, I smelled pancakes! The sight and delicious aroma of those blueberry pancakes made me restless as I sat at the table, but I forced myself to fold my hands for her prayer. Thankfully, her grace was quicker than Grandfather's. Starting on my third cake, drenched in butter and honey, I shared my appreciation. "These pancakes are delicious, Miss Rachel, absolutely delectable! My friend Gio has never eaten blueberries, never once in his life. I've never even seen them at any fruit vendor."

Miss Rachel's soft smile was different that morning—she looked preoccupied, maybe even worried.

"And I'm also thankful, Miss Rachel, that your God accepts shorter graces than Grandfather's God. I'd have an especially hard time waiting through his prayers when I'm smelling your cooking."

110

"My God as compared to your Grandfather's God?" she asked with a puzzled look.

"Yes, there's a pretty clear difference as I see it. Your God is kind and gentle, like your hands when they are healing. Grandfather's God is stronger, like power in the ocean when a storm is rising, and rather scary."

"Oh, Tom Timothy, there is only one true God. Your grandfather and I worship the same all-powerful deity. He is both kind and powerful, loving and righteous, gentle and mighty. He is a God that condemns evil but loves sinners."

Sounded like a bit of a paradox to me, and I told her so.

She leaned forward; her hands clasped. "Yes, Tom Timothy, to humans like us, weak and mortal, God is an almost unfathomable being. He is so great that it is hard for us to comprehend. He created the universe, the moon and stars, and He created us, in His image. To think that an omniscient (all-knowing), omnipotent (all-powerful), and omnipresent (here, there, and everywhere at the same time) God would care about us, about you and me and every human being on this earth, makes little sense. But because He is a God of unlimited love, He does. And because He is perfect, unlike us, He hates evil and sin. He just cannot tolerate it." Miss Rachel sat back.

I liked those omni words—I'd definitely put them in my journal. They were worth pondering.

"But Grandfather says that we are all sinners, flawed on either the inside, outside, or both. Why would such an incredible God want us? I wouldn't if I were him! I'd be totally disgusted with most people, their anger and their violence, their lies and their spitting." (It was hard to get the image of that Mr. Gagnon out of my mind. What God would care about him?)

"Do you know who Jesus is?"

"Yes, he's a character from ancient stories in the Bible. The Irish kids at school mention his name at times, especially when they are surprised. They say, 'Jesus, Mary, and Joseph!' so I guess they're talking about the Christmas group."

"Haven't you read the Bible with your grandfather?"

"Oh, yes. I've read of battles and kings, a special king named David. Grandfather says we will read more when I'm ready. I'm just not all that interested yet. I mean, it's a really old book, and I'm enjoying Zane Grey right now. Good cowboys, gunslingers, villains, deserts, mountains, and a

111

man wrestling buffalo—I like those stories, and they're easier to read than some of the books Grandfather gives me."

"Yes, the battle of good against evil, Tom Timothy, that is one of the oldest truths in the world, and it came directly from God and His Word. It is a central theme throughout the entire Bible. Now you might want to try the New Testament—I think you are ready. You should mention it to your grandfather when he comes home."

Now that reminded me! "When is Grandfather coming home, Miss Rachel?" I asked.

As she opened her mouth to answer me, a sharp knock sounded on her front door. We went together to answer it, and the sight of Mr. Vann, from the general store, frightened us both into silence.

"Telegram, Rachel," he said thrusting the envelope into her hands. Then he tipped his Western Union cap, nodded politely, and hurried back to his truck.

------

1. Zane Grey (1872-1939) was an incredibly successful and prolific American writer of Western adventures. His descriptions were lavish and his heroes more than life-sized. It is interesting that Grandfather would have a copy of one of his books—perhaps it belonged to Tom Timothy's father.

CHAPTER 27

 aine

Miss Rachel's hands shook a little as she quickly opened it. The telegram was angled away from me, so I couldn't read it, though I did try. A sigh escaped her lips, and she put her hand on my shoulder and directed me back to my breakfast. My appetite was gone.

She sat back at the table; her bright black eyes glittered. "Good news Your grandfather is coming home tomorrow, Tom Timothy, so we need to finish up our work here today." She smiled but still looked a little bit sad. "Are you finished with your breakfast?"

"Yes, ma'am. But let me clean up—I always clean up when Grandfather cooks."

"Thank you. I'm going to air out the linens for the guest room then." She stood up and walked away, leaving the folded telegram on the table.

The telegram dared me, tempted me more than all the fruit in Brooklyn. I hungered to have some answers, and I knew there must be some on that paper. Making sure Miss Rachel had gone out to the back garden, I grabbed it and read.

113

Coming to you tomorrow. Be prepared. J

I DROPPED IT, more frustrated than ever, but it stuck to my fingers—the honey! I could only hope Miss Rachel would be too busy to notice the wrinkles and honey stains. I heard her footsteps returning, so I cleared the table quickly.

I washed those dishes with a bit more splashing than necessary. Grandfather's penny-pinching was going to push me over the edge. A few more words of explanation wouldn't have cost but a nickel more! Be prepared for what? I knew it wasn't Miss Rachel's fault that Grandfather was so cryptic, so mysterious, but once again, I was on the outside. I kept my back straight and dried the plates and forks, taking my time and hoping she'd find more chores to do.

When I finally turned around, Miss Rachel stood, holding up the sticky telegram, just looking at me. Her right eyebrow was slightly raised, and she said, "Well, Tom Timothy, did it make you feel any better?"

I knew I turned red; I felt my face heat up. I finally stammered, "No, ma'am."

She waited silently. She didn't look angry, just disappointed, and that was even worse.

"Well, it's not really my fault. You left it on the table, right in front of me." I started to defend myself, but a look of sadness clouded her face, so I stopped. I saw the same look in her eyes as I'd seen in Father's when I'd lied to him about tearing out the pages of his book. Shaking his head, Father had told me that a man's honor is a precious treasure, but lies and deceit would quickly tarnish it, make it worthless. "Don't throw away my trust with empty excuses, son; don't let lies turn your honor to dirt."

"I'm sorry, Miss Rachel." My voice was no stronger than a whisper. I looked at the floor, the telegram, the table, anywhere but in her eyes. Waiting in her silence was more than uncomfortable; it was actually painful as I remembered all her kindnesses. I felt sick when I realized that I had repaid her healings and compassion with treachery. I couldn't fool myself—I was wrong, just plain wrong. Had I lost her friendship forever? She was a part of the family of my heart, like Gio. I took a deep breath and held it for a bit. Then I looked into her eyes. "I'm so sorry, Miss Rachel. Truly. I knew it was wrong, I know it was wrong, but I gave in. I gave in." I dropped my eyes and my head. Everything felt so heavy and dark to me.

She must have moved silently because I was so surprised when I felt her hugging me. "I forgive you, Tom Timothy. Honesty is so important, honesty to others and to yourself. We all sin, do and say what we know we shouldn't, but you are right and wise to admit it. Excuses are like spreading barn muck over a beautiful picture or mud on a clean window. They hide the glory of God and His truths."

The room felt lighter after her words and hug. I was able to look at her again without the weight. It must have been the weight of guilt, like the pilgrim Christian's burden of sin that he carried as a heavy pack on his back[1]. Yes, I'm certain that was guilt, but I'll verify it with Grandfather when he comes home, if I feel brave enough.

"Well, Tom Timothy, that grandfather of yours is certainly enigmatic; it means puzzling. I guess I'd better prepare, whatever that might mean." Miss Rachel was smiling again.

I nodded. "It seems to me that it might have something to do with your healing skills, don't you think? You know Grandfather always comes straight to you when I'm hurt."

"I think you might be right, Tom Timothy. Let's prepare the house to offer solace, comfort, and relief. I'll make sure I have enough herbs, and you can build up the fire first thing in the morning, please, to make sure the rooms are warm enough. I'll need your strength to move the guest bed toward the window. The sun's light is always a great help in healing."

She needed my help—that was good. I thought our friendship was still strong, but I needed one more favor.

"Miss Rachel, I know Grandfather is coming home tomorrow, but the telegram sounds like he is coming here first. Please, may I be here to welcome him?" My stomach hurt as I waited for her answer.

"Yes, Tom Timothy. I will need your help. Your grandfather might be exhausted from all his traveling, and I know he has missed you. But you must follow my directions, no matter what; can you do that?"

"Of course!"

I worked the rest of the day with a smile inside me. I was strong and needed. I wasn't just a kid getting in the way. We went extra early to milk the cows and collect the eggs the next morning– neither of us wanted Grandfa-

115

ther to arrive ahead of us. It was strange; my excitement about Grandfather's return wiped away any fear of moose!

By noon, Miss Rachel's home was ready: a warm fire blazed, the table decorated with pinecones and bright autumn leaves among the white birch branches, the guest bed angled to catch the sun's rays. The rich smell of her herbs filled the rooms with a deep freshness.

"Tom Timothy, when your grandfather arrives, I want you to stay in the house, or at least on the porch. I'm not sure what he will need, so I'll go out to the truck. Can you do that?"

"Yes," I agreed willingly. I'd wait on the porch.

Miss Rachel worked in the kitchen, making her special lavender tea, and I sat before the fire reading. I'd begun one of her favorite books, Great Expectations,[2] and I was glad of the distraction. The trials of Pip made my life look even better—Grandfather's sternness was certainly preferable to being brought up by hand, smacked around and constantly criticized. I felt blessed.

Then the sound of the truck pulled me out of the England in my head, and Miss Rachel quickly wiped her hands and dropped the tea towel to the sink. She looked at me as she hurried to the door. "Only on the porch, Tom Timothy, only on the porch."

I put the book on the edge of the hearth, away from the warming flames, and hurried to the porch. It was Grandfather! He was bent over, talking with Miss Rachel, his hands on her shoulders. He shook his head for a moment, then looked over to me. He nodded, a sad smile barely visible above his beard, and raised his hand to keep me where I was.

They walked around the truck, and Grandfather carefully opened the door. He reached in, but I couldn't see what he was doing. Miss Rachel stood beside him, her hands clasped as though in prayer.

As Grandfather backed away from the truck, I first saw feet, then a body in his arms. I could tell from the shoes and skirt that it was a girl. Grandfather held her easily as she looked very skinny and frail. She must be hurt— and for some reason, the thought of that wounded seal came to my mind. Would Grandfather pray again? Could Miss Rachel heal her? Miss Rachel moved forward and laid her hand on the girl's head. I knew how cool and soft her hand would feel. Grandfather came slowly forward, and the sun broke through the clouds and shone on him. I couldn't see her face, but the light lit up her hair, brown and curly. Brown and curly like mine.

I couldn't have moved even if I hadn't promised not to. Miss Rachel hurried to me, wrapping an arm around my shaking body, pulling me close while Grandfather carried her toward me. He turned to the side, and then I saw her face, so pale and still.

"Mother?"

She didn't open her eyes.

---

1. Reference to John Bunyan's allegory *The Pilgrim's Progress.* Tom Timothy read the classic work and discussed it with his grandfather during *Boyo,* the first book in this series
2. Charles Dickens's famous coming-of-age story that focuses on the character Pip as he grows up. Tom Timothy is referring to Pip's abusive childhood where physical punishment was very common.

ABOUT THE AUTHOR

With decades of teaching experience from middle school through college, master teacher and educator Dr. Amy Hodgson is committed to creating thought-provoking and inspiring works that not only delight but also educate the reader. You can find her literary courses at www.DiscernAcademy.com.